WRITER'S RETWEET

PIERS ANTHONY

www.dreamingbigpublications.com

CONTENTS

Introduction

When things went wrong with traditional publishing, I moved on to self publishing. That is, I went to a company that facilitated self publishing, so I wouldn't have to struggle with every detail myself. I'm a writer, not a publisher. This meant no advance payments, no big promotional budget, and I had to pay for things like covers. I could no longer get mass market paperback editions, which had been the mainstay of my success. It was now mostly electronic. But I had pretty much complete control. No editor could pick and choose, rejecting my best work in favor of what he thought was more commercial. No copy editor could substitute her notion of proper English usage for mine. I have a BA in Creative Writing, over fifty years' experience as a commercial author, and was once an English teacher. I get annoyed when my correct usage gets overruled in favor of error by someone who wasn't born when I started selling fiction. I had freedom at last. So there were tradeoffs, but on the whole I was satisfied.

The self publisher asked me to provide a series of Tweets as a promotional device. That is, little messages, each limited to 140 characters or less. Now I am old, and I come from another century; these newfangled gimmicks are for the birds. Indeed, to me a tweet is something a little bird says as it looks for a place to deposit its droppings. Saying something meaningful in such short measure is problematical. So I was somewhat at a loss.

Then I got a notion: suppose I told a story in tweets? Each individual tweet might be beneath notice, like a bird dropping, but a few hundred of them could add up to fertilizer for some real poop.

Thus came to be my series of tweeted stories. I understand fans liked them, but of course it was hard to get the whole thing one tweet at a time. So now I have collected the five stories I did piecemeal into one volume, and anyone who was frustrated about missing sections before can get the whole story now.

I tracked the tweets by labeling each a chapter, coded by my initials, the story, and the chapter. The first one started out like this:

PA1ch1 This is the story of a man and a

mystery, titled "Experiment," told in Tweet chapters designated PA1ch1, PA1ch2 etc.; track them. [Okay, I edited out part of that as no longer relevant.]

PA1ch2 Once upon a time, in a universe near ours, there lived and worked a man who thought he was beneath notice.

But this would become tedious after a few seconds. So for this volume I have deleted the tweet structure and formatted the stories conventionally. There are still some minor problems. For example, to maintain clarity with one line a day I had to identify characters often, and that can become annoying in an all together text. But I wanted to keep the same wording, so I hope readers will tune it out or suffer through.

So what did I find to write? First I wanted something dramatic enough to attract and hold a person one day at a time; philosophical depth was unnecessary. So for "Experiment" I made a really dull character who gets thrust into a really wild adventure. You know, like a typical reader discovering one of my books. That's humor; I prefer to think of my readers as superior folk with excellent taste. I developed that through three short stories. When that was done I was working in my back yard clearing out the chronic weedy overgrowth, getting sweaty and scratched and all, not really enjoying it. I wondered what it would take to make it interesting, and that led to the slightly naughty story "Dull Street Incident." Finally I did a novelette, "Strange Fruit," that starts with an odd fruit in a refrigerator and leads to something like Heaven and Hell.

No need to bore you any further with incidental commentary. Get on into the stories, and I hope they make your own dull life more interesting.

"Experiment"

  This is the story of a man and a mystery, titled "Experiment," told in Tweet chapters.

  Once upon a time, in a universe near ours, there lived and worked a man who thought he was beneath notice. He was not particularly smart, handsome or rich. He had hair-colored hair, blue-brown eyes, and a barely average nose. His name was Bigelow Bilge, but we will call him Bigelow. He gave ordinary a bad name.

  Naturally, Bigelow's prospects for fame, wealth, or even romance were scant. He was bored with his dull job and his duller life. As Bigelow walked home from the subway stop Friday afternoon, little did he know how drastically all that was about to change. Had he but known his near future, he might still have lacked the imagination or the fortitude to change it.

Suddenly a heavy safe crashed onto the pavement barely two feet ahead of him. One more stride and he would have been flattened.

Bigelow gaped stupidly at the mass of metal. Sheer blind luck had saved him from being lethally squished. Which was weird, because luck had never been kind to him before. Had the cosmos made an error?

He looked around, but there was no one else in sight. No one had witnessed his narrow escape. He was almost disappointed. It was, after all, just about Bigelow's only possible claim to fame: almost getting squelched by a falling safe.

He looked up into the sky. Tall buildings rose on either side, but none overhung this spot. So where had the safe fallen from?

Bigelow shook his head. Was he losing his indifferent mind? How could a heavy safe fall from nowhere and almost pulp him? Something was distinctly weird here. But he couldn't dally indefinitely pondering the senselessness of it. Bigelow stepped around that fallen safe and resumed his walk toward his completely unremarkable rented apartment. He was looking forward to another dull pre-fab frozen meal, the kind suitable for incompetent single men.

A speeding car whipped around a corner, heading right toward him. Bigelow threw himself to the side barely in time. The car zoomed on, never even swerving to avoid him, never pausing. It seemed it didn't care what it hit.

Bigelow had just suffered another impossibly narrow escape from death. What the bleep was going on here?!

Now Bigelow was eager to get on to his dull home base. At least he would be safe there. Then he could forget these scares. He picked himself up, dusted himself off, and resumed walking.

A stray dog came out from behind a trash barrel. Bigelow did not care one way or another about stray dogs. But this one looked strange. Foam showed on its muzzle.

Uh-oh. Maybe the dog had been into foamy trash. But this one was eyeing him with what looked like rage. In fact it looked like a rabid dog. Bigelow did not like this at all. If the mad animal charged—

The rabid dog charged. Bigelow knew that one bite, one scratch, could infect him with rabies. Bigelow threw himself to the side, just as he had with the rogue car. The charging dog just missed him. He scrambled for the nearest alley. He launched himself up the first fire escape. Panting, he looked down and back.

The rabid dog was gone. It must have given up the chase when it saw Bigelow pull himself up out of reach.

Bigelow had just survived a third deadly threat in as many minutes. His heart was pounding. Had the world gone crazy?

He climbed cautiously down from the fire escape, alert for the mad dog, but it did not reappear. Someone else's misfortune? Bigelow went to the end of the alley and peered out onto the street. Nothing. Was it safe to resume his walk home?

He nerved himself, took a deep breath, and put a foot forward. And paused, because he heard something ominous. There was a sound above him, as of something crumbling. He looked up. Part of the wall was coming loose over his head. In fact it was detaching from the building and tumbling down toward him. He barely pulled back before it crashed where he had been.

That was Escape #4. Now Bigelow knew something was going on. But what? Was fate itself trying to eliminate him?

He hurried down the alley, not venturing back into the dangerous street. These narrow escapes were beyond coincidence. But he was a completely unremarkable man. Why should anything remarkable ever happen to him? It did not make sense.

As Bigelow approached the far end of the alley, he saw flames and smoke. There must have been an accident that caught fire. At least this one was not happening right where he stood. He had time to avoid it. But he was trapped in the alley.

He checked the buildings on either side. In a

moment he found a door. Maybe it was the exit of a restaurant or something. Bigelow tried the door handle. To his surprise it turned; it was unlocked. He opened the door and stepped into the building.

He stood in a small hall leading to an elevator. But he didn't want that; he wanted safely out. So he passed it by.

The door ahead of him opened suddenly. A young woman entered. She saw him and hesitated. "Uh, hello," Bigelow said.

"Oh, you're real!" she said, seeming relieved. Then she reconsidered. "Or are you?"

Bigelow was taken aback. "I am real, as far as I know. But the past few minutes have been exceedingly odd."

"Let me touch you," she said, approaching. Bigelow, surprised again, merely stood there. She touched his sleeve.

"I'm afraid I don't understand," Bigelow said. "Am I not supposed to be real? My name is Bigelow Bilge, short for Bilgewater."

"I am Paula Plain, short for Plaintiff." She smiled, and that greatly improved her aspect. They shook hands. "You see," Paula continued, "I have recently been beset by nasty illusions. I needed to be sure you weren't another."

"Illusions?" Bigelow asked, having a nasty suspicion. "I just escaped several remarkable threats.

I wonder—"

"So it's happening to you too!" Paula said. "Oh, that's such a relief! I mean, I'm sorry you're suffering, but it really helps me."

"You thought you were losing your mind?" Bigelow asked. "I thought I was being attacked. Are they really illusions?"

Paula smiled again. Bigelow really liked that. "We can verify it. What did you last see?"

"A fire in the street. After a falling safe, a rogue car, a rabid dog, and a crumbling wall. I was really scared."

She took his hand. He *really* liked that. "Let's go see your fire. I believe I can prove it is illusion."

They went to the door he had entered by. They exited the building, still holding hands. Of course that meant nothing; still...

Still, it meant that he had to hold the door open for Paula while she slid past him. Her modest bosom just brushed his chest. That was closer to romantic contact than Bigelow had been in years, even if it was purely coincidental. He knew it didn't mean anything. But he was secretly thrilled anyway. To be this close to a real live girl!

Then they were outside. Bigelow was almost afraid that the fire would be gone, but it was still burning brilliantly.

"Where is it?" Paula asked, peering both ways

down the alley. "Where's the fire?"

"You don't see it?" Bigelow asked. "It's right at the end, that way." He pointed toward the fire.

Paula looked that way again. "I don't see it," she said. "Don't worry; I do believe you. This merely proves something significant."

"It does?" Bigelow asked, feeling moderately stupid. "You're not seeing what I see proves something?"

"Yes," Paula said. "It proves that the illusions are specific to each of us. I don't see yours, and I'm sure you won't see mine."

"Uh, okay," Bigelow said. Mainly he was pleased that she was still holding his hand. "Should we go there?"

"Definitely," Paula said. "Come on!" She tugged him along after her, walking toward the fire.

They came to the fire. Bigelow heard the crackle of it and felt the heat. If this was illusion, it was mighty convincing.

"You're still seeing the fire?" Paula asked. "It hasn't faded out? Please answer honestly; this is important."

"It's still there," Bigelow agreed. "It's really hot. I'll get burned if I go much closer."

"Then this should really impress you," Paula said. She let go of his hand, then walked straight into the blaze.

"Watch out!" Bigelow cried. But he was too late. Paula was already in the fire, walking through the flames.

And the flames weren't hurting her. They wrapped around her slender body and sifted through her brown hair, harmlessly.

Paula turned, standing in the middle of the fire. "You see, for me there is nothing. It's your illusion, not mine."

Bigelow had to believe it. The fire, real as it seemed to him, was not affecting her at all. Paula stood completely untouched.

"Now you can come to me," she said. "To demonstrate that it *is* illusion. That it can't really hurt you."

But Bigelow hesitated. "That blaze is awfully real to me. I hate to look like a coward, but I don't have the nerve to risk it."

"That's all right," Paula said, coming toward him. "My illusions terrify me too. But let's try something else."

"Something else?"

Paula came right up to Bigelow. She took his hand. "Will you trust me?" she asked. He nodded, uncertain what she had in mind.

"Close your eyes," Paula told him. "Let me lead you blind." When he hesitated, she leaned close and kissed him briefly. "Please."

Bigelow closed his eyes. What else could he do? He was mesmerized by the kiss. No woman had ever done that before.

"Keep them closed," Paula said. She led him on. All he was conscious of was her soft little hand in his, and her faint perfume.

After a short distance they stopped. "Now look," Paula said, letting go of his hand. "Look back the way we just came."

Bigelow looked. There was the fire, behind them. Could he really have walked right through it, hearing and feeling nothing?

"Now do you want to try it with your eyes open?" Paula asked. She took his hand again and led him toward the fire.

Bigelow hesitated. Would Paula be mad if he balked? Or, more importantly, would she kiss him again if he cooperated? He decided to cooperate. He followed Paula toward the fire. He felt its rising heat, but he kept going. They stepped into the fire. And it didn't burn him! It was all around him, fiercely blazing, but it wasn't hurting him. Bigelow stopped in the middle of the fire. "It really is illusion!" he exclaimed. "I see it, but am not being touched."

"Yes!" Paula agreed gladly. She flung her arms about him and kissed him again. Then she drew back. "Sorry. I got carried away."

"That's all right," Bigelow said. "I—" He

paused, gathering his gumption. "I liked it." Would that turn her off?"

"You're nice," Paula said. "I'll try not to embarrass you again. I just wanted to prove to you that we are dealing with illusions."

"You proved it," Bigelow said. "But that only raises big questions. Who or what is doing this to us, and why?"

"Exactly my question," Paula agreed as they walked on down the street. "Let alone the technology required. How—" She froze.

"What's the matter," Bigelow asked. "Why are you standing there looking as if you are seeing a ghost?"

"Because I *am* seeing a ghost," Paula said. "Or at least an illusion. There's a coiled rattlesnake in front of me."

Bigelow saw nothing. "Not for me. It's definitely illusion. Evidently programmed for you, not for me."

"Yes," Paula agreed. "But a terrifying one. I hate snakes! I know most of them are harmless, and all that, but I can't go near one."

"Then maybe I can help you," Bigelow said gallantly. "Take my hand, close your eyes. I'll lead you past it."

"Yes," Paula agreed faintly. "I made you do it. Now it's my turn." She paused shivering. "But oh,

I'm terrified!"

Bigelow took her hand. Paula closed her eyes. Then he led her forward, right through where the snake might be. After a suitable distance, he stopped. "I think it's safe now."

Paula opened her eyes and looked back. She shuddered. "That rattler is still there, ringing its bell," Paula said. "But when I walked with you, eyes closed, I heard nothing."

"That seems to be the way it works," Bigelow said. "It is primarily sight oriented. When you tune that out, the rest fades too."

"Yes," Paula agreed. "So now we can counter it, with each other's help. But there's still the question of who is doing it."

"I see maybe two options," Bigelow said. "One is to do the opposite of what the illusions are trying to make us do."

"So maybe after a while they'll give it up as a bad job," Paula agreed. "And leave us alone. Maybe together."

"I wouldn't mind that," Bigelow said. "If you wouldn't." He waited, fearing that she would angrily refute the notion.

Paula considered. Then she smiled. "Your place or mine?" But then she reconsidered. "What is your other option?"

"To go where they are evidently driving us,

up that elevator, and take the bull by the horns, as it were. Then we'll know."

She considered again. "I like the way your mind works. Why were two rather ordinary people like us chosen for this?"

"My guess is it's an experiment of some sort. To see how well their system works. We're of no account; safe to try it on, maybe."

"To see how well they can herd us," she agreed. "If it works on us, then they can refine it for more important folk."

"Maybe it's a secret government project," Bigelow said. "Maybe if it works, they'll need to hire more hands to run it."

"Like us!" Paula agreed. "My job is so dull I can't stand it. I'd love some adventure." She turned her eyes to him. "And maybe—"

Bigelow nerved himself and said it: "And some romance. If I had a girl who was interested."

Paula smiled. "You have one, Bigelow. I might not have noticed you on the street, but after this experience, I'm in."

Bigelow's heart was thumping for joy. "Then shall we go brace the lion's den, together?"

"Let's." Then she thought of something. "After this." She put her arms around him and kissed him firmly on the mouth. Then, together, holding hands, they marched into the alley, heedless of any more illusions.

"DISCOVERY"

First there was a falling safe that barely missed him, then a car that almost ran him down, then a rabid dog. What was going on? Trying to escape a collapsing wall, then a fire in the street, Bigelow opened a convenient door and entered a hall. There he met a young woman, Paula Plain, who had been driven here by similar illusions. Illusions? The threats weren't real?

The two of them verify that these are targeted illusions that no one else can see. She can't see his fire, or he her rattlesnake. They help each other get past their illusions. They are sight and sound, not substance. They can be safely ignored.

But who is doing this to them, and why? They decide to go where the illusions lead, and find out.

And they kiss. Because they like each other. Neither was interesting enough for romance, before, but they are together in this adventure. So, together, holding hands, Bigelow and Paula march back to where the illusions are herding them.

That completes the original story, for those readers who didn't see it before. Tough luck, for those who did read it.

"I'm scared," Paula said. "Do you really think this is wise?" She was actually rather pretty in her uncertainty.

"No. I think it's foolhardy," he said. "The kind of thing I never did in real life. Which means—"

"Which means we'd better do it," she agreed. "Because otherwise we're both locked in our nonentity."

"Yes. But we don't *have* to do it. Not if you don't want to. There are other ways to find excitement."

She looked at him. "Other ways?" Then she blushed. "You mean—Romance?"

"Well..." Then he blushed. "Not if you don't want to," he repeated, with a changed context. "I just thought—never mind."

"But I'm so skinny!" she protested, looking down at herself. She really needed reassurance.

"Slender," he said. Actually she was thin, but it hardly mattered whether she was thick or thin. She liked him, and he liked her.

"And I'm not beautiful, or sexy, or smart, or anything," she said. "I'm the original wallflower. I'm not worth your while."

Bigelow surprised himself by doing something way beyond his social competence. He kissed her.

Paula kissed him back. "Oh!" she said. "I guess that shuts me up. I just meant that—"

"I'm not handsome or smart or anything either," he said. "You're just right for me."

Her blush deepened. "Do you really want to—to go to my apartment? Now?"

Bigelow was sorely tempted. But several things held him back. "I'd really like to," he said carefully. "But—"

"But we have to see about braving the lion's den first, or we'll never do it," she said. "I reluctantly agree."

That had not been his thought. He was concerned about not measuring up to whatever expectations she might have. But it would do. "Onward to the lion's den," he agreed. They resumed walking.

"That dialogue," Paula said. "It reminds me of something. But it's not exactly relevant. Sometimes I make these obscure connections."

They had been talking about love. Suddenly he was intensely curious about what she was thinking of. "What is it?"

"Well, it was in some magazine, about how during World War Two, married American soldiers were getting interested in British girls. And of course their wives didn't like that. 'What do those girls have that we don't have?' they asked. 'Nothing,' the men replied. 'But they've got it *here*.'" She smiled a bit wistfully. "I've got nothing, but I've got it here."

Bigelow wasn't sure whether to laugh. He didn't want to agree that she had nothing. "That's cute. But you do have something."

"Thank you. But I think that's the point, as you said before. We're pretty much nothing, so they can experiment on us."

"Except that maybe now we have figured it out, so we're not being blindly herded anymore."

They were approaching the door into the building. Bigelow paused. "I wonder if there are others?"

"Others? Oh, you mean other victims? I mean subjects. We can't be the only ones, can we?"

"I should think if it's an experiment, they would want to have a number of subjects. Because people can react differently."

Paula nodded. "Yes. We reacted differently, and were able to help each other get past our particular illusions."

"Maybe they are being staggered," Bigelow said. "That is, a new one started every ten minutes, so they don't bang into each other."

"But we banged into each other," Paula reminded him. "So to speak." She colored slightly, remembering their kisses.

"How fast were you herded? If you went right along, instead of fighting as I did, you could have caught up to me."

"I was pretty fast," she agreed "I mean, being herded. I just wanted to get away from the threats."

"So we could have been staggered," he said. He smiled. "And not just by the kiss."

"Not just by the kisses," she agreed. "Let's do another, just to be sure."

He gazed at her. She had a thin body, a modest bosom, brown hair, and faded brown eyes. She was beautiful.

"But only if you want to," she said quickly. "I don't mean to be pushy. I'm not a pushy person. I'm more like a mouse."

"I was admiring you," Bigelow said quickly. "You're absolutely lovely." Then before she could protest, he kissed her soundly.

She melted in his arms. "No man ever lied to me like that before. Thank you." Then she disengaged. "Time to go, if we're going to."

"This isn't over," he said. "But yes, we can't afford to dally any longer. But after this I think I'll fall in love with you."

"If you do, I'll do it too." Then they opened the door and entered the hall, half expecting to find another person there. But there was only the elevator.

Bigelow paused. "Let me check something." He went to the far door and opened it.

Sure enough, there was a big hairy caveman with a club bearing down on him. He shut the door in the brute's face. "The illusions are still herding us," he said. "I just wanted to be sure. Before we do what they want."

"Of course," Paula agreed. "We were so busy talking, and stuff, that we tuned out the illusions."

They went to the elevator, which was open, and stepped inside. It immediately started rising.

"I'm frightened again," Paula said. "We really don't know what to expect when we get there."

"Whatever it is, it shouldn't be too bad," Bigelow said. "Why should they take so much trouble to herd us, if they mean harm?"

"To see if we are smart enough to escape?" she suggested timorously. "Or too stupid to catch on?"

"We're neither smart nor stupid," he said. "We were selected to be ordinary."

"That's why we were chosen!" Paula agreed. "Because we are so dull nobody notices us." She frowned. "But how do they do it?"

"They must be focusing a beam on us, to project the illusions," Bigelow said. "That means they can see us."

"How?" Paula asked. "I don't see any mobile cameras around. And why are they specific to each of us?"

"No cameras," Bigelow agreed. "So there must be receivers in us, somehow, to get our particular illusions."

"I don't remember getting anything put into me," she said. "I think I would have known if someone poked into me."

Bigelow repressed a wicked thought about how he would like to poke into her. "Except maybe a doctor."

"Or an eye test!" she exclaimed, lovely in her animation. "I had a free eye/ear test last month. Did you?"

"Actually I did," Bigelow said, remembering. "It was pretty thorough. They said my eyes and ears were fine."

"Me too. I didn't need glasses or a hearing aid, so they couldn't sell me any. Yet they didn't seem disappointed."

"Because those tur—um, jerks weren't really trying to sell anything. They were implanting receivers for illusions."

"I think your first word is better," she said. "Those turds were making us involuntary volunteers in their experiment."

"Isn't that an oxymoron?" he asked. "Involuntary volunteer? But I see what you mean. That's when it happened."

"It's the army volunteer system I read about," she said. "I need three volunteers: you, you and you."

Bigelow laughed a bit hollowly. "That's the system all right. I guess they didn't ask because that would ruin the surprise."

"The wonderful surprise of being threatened by a falling safe or a rattlesnake or a fire," Paula agreed.

"So this is either illegal or super-secret," Bigelow concluded. "We'll soon be finding out." He paused. "How about—"

"My thought exactly," she said, stepping into his arms for a kiss. "While we have a bit of privacy, maybe."

"Oh, Paula!" he said. "They may be turds, but they did us the huge favor of putting us together. That makes it all worth it."

"I agree," she said, squeezing his bottom. She laughed when he jumped. So he squeezed hers. It was nicer than his.

Then the elevator shuddered to a halt and its door slid open. They gazed into what was obviously an office, with desks and chairs.

Paula screamed. Because there on the floor were the corpses of a man and a woman. Blood was spreading across the tiles.

Piers Anthony

Bigelow was appalled. But then he caught on. "It's illusion! Sent to both of us. To see if we really understand what's happening."

"Oh, of course," Paula agreed faintly. "Because if we understand, we'll just walk through them into the office. And pass the test."

"So let's pass that test," Bigelow said, taking her hand. They stepped out of the elevator together.

And tripped over the bodies. They fell on them, so weren't hurt. "They're real!" Paula said, horrified. "And still warm."

"Still warm," he echoed as they scrambled to get off the bodies and onto their feet, slightly blood smeared.

Paula rummaged in her handbag and brought out a damp wipe. She scrubbed Bigelow's pant legs to get the blood off. He would have protested, but realized that this little domestic favor was probably keeping her from freaking out. "Thanks." Meanwhile he had a worse concern. "Suppose we get blamed for this? Are we being framed for murder?"

"Murder!" Paula exclaimed, shocked. But then she had a better notion. "The illusions started before these people were killed."

"So it can't be a plot," Bigelow agreed, relieved. "Not against us. But then, why were these folk killed?"

"I think I know!" Paula exclaimed. "Another subject got here before us, and was so mad about it

30

that he killed them and fled."

"That must be it," Bigelow agreed. "He got scared out of his wits, herded here, learned it was all an experiment—"

"And blew his top," Paula said. "He just went crazy. And knifed them to death." She smiled. "He was not amused."

"And now we're stuck holding the bag," Bigelow said "What are we going to do? So we don't get blamed?"

"Flee before they know we're here?" Paula asked plaintively. It was obvious that this was hope rather than conviction.

"They have to know we're here," Bigelow said. "They've been tracking us, so they know when to throw their illusions at us."

"Yes, of course," she agreed. "So they must know who was here before us, too. Still, I think we're in a picklement."

"A kosher dill picklement," he agreed. "But look, we wanted adventure. Now's our chance. Let's contact them about this."

"Yes!" she agreed, and kissed him. "I'll try to call them now. They must be wondering why their people stopped communicating."

They went to the desk. There was a TV screen showing a map of the city, with half a dozen red dots on it.

There was also a red telephone. "I'll put it on Speaker," Paula said. "So we can both talk to them." She touched a button. "Hello," Paula said. "We need to talk to someone in authority. Please answer."

"Provide your access code," a man's voice answered. That was all.

"We don't have an access code," Paula said. "We're not your regular operators. We need your help." But there was no response. "Please, we can't do anything without your help," Paula pleaded. "We have no idea what's going on. Please."

There was still no response. That annoyed Bigelow, partly because it wasn't courteous, mostly because Paula was frustrated. That made Bigelow mad "Listen, you smuck," he snapped. "Your folk here have been brutally slaughtered and it's a bloody mess here." He took a breath. "We didn't do it, and we're ready to help if we can. But we need your help in return." He took another breath. "So stop this crap about access codes and talk to us. Otherwise we'll leave and take it to the nearest police station." One more breath. "And let them damn well sort it out. I'll give you a count of ten to answer before we go." Still no response. So he started counting. "Ten. Nine. Eight, Seven, Six, Five. Four. Three."

Suddenly the phone spoke. "Acknowledged. Our apology for the delay. Please identify yourselves."

"Bigelow and Paula," Bigelow said, thrilled

with his victory. "You have us in your records, no? Look us up."

"Welcome to the Project, Mr. Bilge and Miss Plain. How may we help you?"

Well now. "Tell us what to do with these bodies. We gather this is a secret operation, so you don't want these murders known."

"You are correct, Mr. Bilge. It is important that secrecy be maintained. We will send a crew to pick them up."

"Good enough. Now tell us what this monitor with the city and dots is for." He gestured at the computer screen, as if that helped.

"That is to track the several remaining subjects. When one goes the wrong way, we send an illusion to turn them back."

Just so. Bigelow could see that Paula was as pleased as he was with their progress. "What do we tell them when they get here?"

There was a brief hesitation. "You thank them for their participation and recruit them to the mission."

"And what is the mission?" Bigelow asked. "It must be pretty important, to warrant all this business."

Another hesitation. "We are not free to divulge that at this time."

"Oh for pity's sake!" Paula said. "How can we do this if we don't know?"

"It is complicated. Regulations do not permit revelation of core data to unauthorized parties."

Bigelow was getting mad again. "Listen, you turd. In World War Two the American soldiers were making out with foreign girls." He took one of his breaths. "When their wives asked what the Brits had that the wives didn't have, know what they answered?"

The voice sounded confused. That was good. "Mr. Bilge, I don't see the relevance. What have British girls to do with—"

"They answered 'Nothing. But they've got it *here.*' See my point? Or do you need it in words of one syllable?"

There was another pause. "I believe I do. You are saying that we need operatives on the spot, right now, and you are there."

"Right. We've got nothing, but we've got it here. So work with us. We're willing and able, if you just tell us how."

"You have a point, Mr. Bilge. Give us a moment to organize our presentation, and we will cooperate with you. We'll call back."

The phone went dead. Paula hugged him. "Wonderful!" she said. "You were so masterful!"

"Well, I never got threatened by falling safes, rabid dogs, and fires before," he said. "I just got mad."

"I love it when you're mad." She kissed him. "And you used my example so well! You're a genius."

"No, I just used what you gave me." But he was ridiculously pleased by her compliment.

"Do you think we have time?" she asked. "'Before they call back?" She glanced around the office, skipping over the bodies.

"Time for what?" But then she was passionately kissing him again, and he realized he was being stupid. "Maybe we do," Bigelow agreed. After all, when would they have more time alone, when things got going?

As it turned out they did have time. Then it got interesting in more than one sense. But that is another story. Stay tuned for "Mission" in due course.

"MISSION"

This commences the third Tweet story, about Bigelow Bilge and Paula Plain, two dull folk who suddenly started wildly hallucinating. He saw a falling safe, a wild car, a rabid dog, all trying to wipe him out. She saw a rattlesnake and others, similarly dangerous. But it turned out they weren't hallucinations. They were projected illusions. Someone was trying to scare them, or drive them somewhere.

They decided to find out, by letting the illusions herd them to a building and an upper room. Where two people had been murdered. It seemed that someone else had gotten there before them, and been pretty annoyed, and gruesomely killed the operators.

Bigelow and Paula had gotten interested in each other in the course of the adventure, in fact they kissed, maybe even more. So they worked together to smoke out the folk who ran this operation, and make them clean up the mess and explain things.

"Mr. Bilge. Ms. Plain," the speakerphone said. "We hereby deputize the two of you as Project Illusion operatives. Do you agree?"

"We do," Bigelow and Paula said almost together. Were they finally about to find out what this was all about? Without illusion?

"You will be added to our payroll and issued appropriate papers. On condition that you keep strict confidence about this matter."

Bigelow exchanged a glance with Paula. She nodded. They had concluded this was a secret operation. "We agree. What's it about?"

"We will answer," the phone said. "But first you must clean up the mess. As members of the group, this is now your responsibility."

"Oh, we have to do your dirty work?" Bigelow asked, bridling. "That's why you were so agreeable to signing us up?"

"Frankly, yes," the phone said. "There is no one else to do it, and more clients will be arriving soon. We need your help."

Bigelow opened his mouth angrily, but Paula put a hand on his arm, shaking her head. "Okay," he said somewhat gruffly. She smiled. That somehow made it worthwhile. Besides, obviously help was needed, and Bigelow and Paula were on the spot. They eyed the bodies.

Then something occurred to Bigelow. "How do you know that *we* didn't murder those folk? We're the only ones here."

"The door camera showed the two of you entering after it happened," the phone said. "We knew you were innocent."

"Did the camera see who really did it?" Paula asked. When there was no immediate answer, she continued. "So you know who did it."

"We do," the phone admitted reluctantly. "But there was nothing we could do about it. We're shorthanded at the moment."

Bigelow looked at the bodies. They had not improved with age. "Where do you want us to put them?" Bigelow asked. "The freezer?"

"Yes, actually. Until we can arrange to have them removed from the premises. There's a large freezer in back. There should be room."

Bigelow had thought he was making a grim joke. But he had never been very good at jokes. They found the mostly empty chest freezer. Then they braced themselves. They took hold of the man's body, one on each arm, and dragged him across the floor to the freezer. Then they wrestled him up onto the open freezer and let his body thunk down into it, flat. It looked as if he were sleeping there. They tackled the woman next. They dragged her to the freezer and dumped her down on top of the man. She landed face down on him.

"Lovers' tryst," Paula said, grimacing. Bigelow winced as he smiled. They closed the lid on the grimly embracing couple. Ugh!

Now they had to clean up the floor. Blood was streaked from the dragging, and pooled in the center where the bodies had been. They got a bucket and mop. Paula knew how to use it, first diluting the blood, then mopping it up and squeezing it into the bucket.

"While we work, tell us about the project," Bigelow said to the phone. "Exactly why does it exist? What do you hope to accomplish?"

"That is an unfortunate story," the phone said. "We got a report that a foreign country was about to attack us with illusions."

"Illusions!" Paula exclaimed. "Like the ones you threw at us? That scared us and finally brought us here, for good or ill?"

"Similar," the phone said. "Only worse. We understand they can project them to anyone, so that several can see the same ones."

"No setting folk up with eye-ear exams?" Bigelow asked. "Like a holographic projection everyone can see at the same time?"

"Yes. That could wreak havoc and maybe be a critical distraction, so that we could be attacked and not be able to defend ourselves."

"That's serious," Bigelow said. "So you set up a small trial group to find out how people would react, so you'd know what to do?"

"Yes. It's very private, because we don't want the unknown enemy to know we're doing it. They might attack sooner, if they knew."

"Only it went wrong," Paula said. Then she paused in her cleanup. "Could the enemy have done it? To mess up any possible defense?"

"That's our fear," the phone said. "Still, the killer was one of our subjects, so probably he acted on his own. This must be quiet."

"We understand," Bigelow said. "But maybe you should have had a guard on duty, to prevent anything like this from happening."

"Yes. But we suffered a budget cut, and are short of personnel. We could afford only those two, and now you. It's difficult."

Before long they had the floor clean. Just in time, because another client was arriving. They heard the footsteps beyond the door.

"Get into your places," the phone said urgently. "You will have to acquaint the next client with the situation, and enlist his silence."

"How?" Paula asked. "He is unlikely to be pleased about the illusions. A handshake probably won't be sufficient."

"In the desk there are citations made out to each participant. Also gift cards for a thousand dollars. That's all we can afford."

They checked the desk and found the citations and cards. It did not seem like much, but it would have to do. Paula organized them.

In a moment the door opened and a nondescript man appeared. He looked across the room at them. "Are you real or illusory?" he asked.

"We are real," Bigelow said. "Congratulations! You have successfully navigated the labyrinth and reached the conclusion."

"The conclusion of what?" the man asked, stepping cautiously into the room. "I was just minding my own business, when—"

"We understand," Paula said. "We suffered similar effects. It was weird and frightening, until we realized they weren't real."

"For sure," the man agreed. "Once I realized I could just close my eyes, I got through. Then I wondered what it was all about."

"So you came here," Bigelow said. "As we did. Well, this is an experiment to determine how ordinary folk like us react."

"Because our government fears that another country is going to attack us using exactly this kind of illusion," Paula said, smiling.

The man took visible stock. "So there is a

reason for this remarkable experience I just suffered? I wasn't just being teased?"

"There was a reason," Bigelow agreed. "As appreciation for your service to our country, you get a citation and a gift card."

"A citation!" the man exclaimed. "I go through a day of doubting my sanity, and I get a citation?" Then he paused. "How much?"

"A thousand dollars," Paula said with her most winning smile, the one that dazzled Bigelow. "But please don't tell how you got it."

"Because we don't want the enemy country to learn that we are on to their foul plot," Bigelow said. "This project is secret."

The man considered. Paula smiled at him again, and he decided to go along. He accepted the citation and card, and departed.

Bigelow and Paula made a joint sign of relief. One down, several to go. "Congratulations," the phone said. "You're real pros."

"I suppose we are, now," Bigelow agreed, pleased. Paula kissed him on the ear. That magnified his pleasure. He patted her butt.

Soon the door opened again. This time it was a nondescript woman. She looked at them, then closed her eyes. They knew why.

"We are not illusions," Bigelow said. "We are real people. Congratulations on successfully navigating the illusions to get here."

"Oh what a relief!" the woman said. "I wasn't completely sure of my sanity. But what's this all about? It has been a nightmare."

They explained things to the woman, and gave her her citation and gift card, and sent her on her way. This was almost routine.

"Trouble," the phone said. "The murderer is returning. He still has his knife." Bigelow and Paula stared at each other, appalled.

"What are we supposed to do?" Bigelow asked. "We don't have any weapons. I'm surprised you don't have a metal alarm set up."

"We do have a metal alarm," the phone said. "But his knife is made of obsidian or ceramics or some other nonmetallic substance."

"So he came fully prepared," Bigelow said. "He knew what he was going to do. He must be a professional killer, or a real fanatic."

"Both, we fear," the phone said. "He will not be easy to handle. Unfortunately there are no weapons of any kind in the office."

"Great," Bigelow muttered. "So what do you recommend? I don't suppose there's a private rear exit so we can escape? A fire escape?"

"Nothing," the phone said. "You will simply have to improvise. We were not prepared for such a savage reaction, and made no plans."

Paula desperately checked through the desk. "Handcuffs!" she exclaimed. "We can put them on him. That will slow him down."

"How?" Bigelow asked. "He's not going to stand there and put his hands behind his back. He'll be coming after us with the knife."

"Maybe I can distract him so you can grab him from behind," Paula said. "By—" She flushed. "By using my, my feminine wiles?"

Bigelow would have protested, but realized it was probably their best chance. If she flashed the man, he might pause long enough.

At any rate, it was their only chance. If they did nothing, they would get knifed to death, just as the prior couple had been.

"I'll wait behind the door," Bigelow said. "You do what you have to do." Paula nodded, and he went to stand to the side of the door.

It burst open and the attacker hurtled into the room, his glossy black knife drawn. He didn't say a word; he simply charged ahead. Bigelow was caught off-guard by the suddenness of the man's action. He stood there for a moment, uncertain what to do.

Fortunately, Paula acted. "Hello, handsome," she said, opening her shirt to show her pink bra. "What can we do for you today?"

Now it was the killer who was taken aback. Obviously he had never expected this kind of welcome. He paused in place.

Bigelow moved quietly up behind the man, holding the handcuffs. But being there wasn't enough; the hands needed to be behind.

Then the killer jumped forward. "You'll do," he said, sheathing his knife and reaching for Paula. "Are you alone?"

"Of course not," Paula said, smiling determinedly. "There's an army on the way here." She removed her shirt and unsnapped her bra.

"You know I'll kill you immediately after," the killer said. "I can't afford to leave witnesses. So I'll have to tie you up first."

"Of course," Paula said. "You can't afford to trust me one minute. I'm your enemy. But you forgot about the man behind you."

"Ha-ha. Old joke," the man said, not laughing. He produced a length of nylon cord. "Now turn around and put your hands behind you."

"Like this?" Paula asked. She raised one hand with a small can. Suddenly spray shot out and caught the man right in the face.

"Oww!" the man cried, clapping his hands to his eyes.

Bigelow immediately jumped forward and snapped one handcuff on one wrist. Then he wrenched the man's other hand around and clapped the other handcuff on. The man's hands were in front, not behind; too bad.

"You did it!" Paula cried. "You captured him!" She grabbed the nylon cord and wrapped it around the man's legs, tying them together.

"You were the one who did it," Bigelow said. "If you hadn't distracted him so effectively, I could not have done anything with him."

"Thank you," Paula said faintly, realizing how exposed she was. She put her bra and shirt back on, somewhat to Bigelow's regret.

"What was that you used on him?" Bigelow asked. "I thought we had no weapons. Was it mace or pepper spray? Something worse?"

"Much worse," she agreed with half a smile. "It was perfume. The atomizer is alcohol based, and can really sting the eyes."

Bigelow sniffed the man, who was recovering. He smelled of sweet violets. Paula's perfume. "Genius!" he exclaimed, laughing.

"If you two idiots are quite done complimenting each other," the killer said sourly, "What are you going to do next? Kill me?"

Bigelow and Paula exchanged a look. They had saved their own lives, but neither had any idea where to go from here. Kill him? Ouch!

"That's what I thought," the man said. "You are amateurs, maybe spot recruited after I terminated the prior pair. You have no idea."

"We'll just have to turn you over to the police," Bigelow said. "They'll know what to do with you. You killed two innocent people."

"Innocent, my eye! They were agents of the government. What I did was an act of war. I'd do it again, if I got the chance."

"What government do you represent?" Paula asked him cannily. "Obviously it's not the one we represent. Who are you, anyway?"

"Why don't you torture me to find out?" the man demanded. He laughed harshly. "You amateurs didn't even take my knife."

Oops! Bigelow hastily removed the man's sheath and knife. But he wondered: why had the man called their attention to it?

"You know we won't torture you," Paula said. "You want to bargain for your freedom. What do you have to offer us?"

"So you're not a total loss, apart from your boobs," the man said. "You've got half a notion where we stand, maybe. Or maybe not."

"What should we do with this guy?" Bigelow asked the phone. "We're amateurs, as he says, while he's a pro. We need advice."

"He also knows we can't afford to turn him over to the police," the phone said. "This project must remain strictly private."

"So the boss is listening in," the man said.

"Good enough. Sure, I'll bargain. My freedom in exchange for some information."

"You can trust us," Paula said. "Because you know we're amateurs, with amateur ideals. But how can we trust your information?"

"Your spook on the phone will be able to verify it as we speak," the man said. "So when he is satisfied, you will let me go free."

"But then you may blab about this project," Bigelow said. "We can't take your word you won't. You know we can't trust you."

"You numb-skull!" the man exclaimed. "I represent the enemy. We already know about the project. I'm here to stop it."

"Oh," Bigelow said, taken aback by his own naïveté. "And I guess you won't be advertising your part in it. You'll just disappear."

"Right. My employer doesn't want the illusion matter publicized any more than yours does, albeit it maybe for a different reason."

"So I guess we have a deal," Bigelow said. "You tell us what we want to know, and we'll turn you loose. But without your knife."

"Deal," the man agreed. "To save time, I'll tell you that everything you need to know is accessible via the master unit. Here."

"You brought it with you?" the phone asked, amazed. "That thing is invaluable. It should be in unbreakable code, locked in a safe."

"There's no such thing as an unbreakable code, dolt," the man said. "And how could I quietly flee the country, towing a big safe?"

So the killer was treating the phone man with the same contempt as Bigelow and Paula. Bigelow was privately amused. "Give it here."

"It's in my pocket, opposite the knife," the man said. "You'll have to fetch it out yourself. I'm indisposed at the moment."

Paula felt in the man's pocket while Bigelow watched closely in case he tried to grab her with his manacled hands. He didn't.

Paula found a small box of featureless hard plastic. It did not look like a disc container. "Is this it?" she asked dubiously.

"That's it, honey," the man said. "Maybe I should make you pay for it with a kiss and a feel. Want to take off your shirt again?"

"No!" Paula snapped, blushing. She held up the box. "How do you open this thing? Is there a key or a sliding panel or something?"

"You don't exactly open it," the man said. "You operate it. This is an operative unit, I think more advanced than your folk have."

"So how do I operate it?" Paula asked, sliding her fingers across the smooth surfaces of the box. "I'm not finding any switches."

"Let me see that," Bigelow said. Paula gave him the box and he ran his fingers over it, but couldn't find any sliding panels.

"Oh, did I forget to mention it is coded?" the man asked with mock regret. "It's keyed to my fingerprints, ignoring all others."

Naturally there was a catch. No wonder the man was not concerned about them getting hold of the device. They couldn't use it.

"We need that information," the phone said. "We can't afford to wait to get it in our laboratory, where it might self destruct."

"You got that right," the man agreed. "Any attempt to pry it open will wipe it out. Isn't that a pity." He smiled nastily.

"So exactly what kind of a deal are you trying to make?" Bigelow asked, nettled. "Why should we free you for this useless thing?"

"You can't use it, but I can," the man said. "I can activate it and make it perform. That's what you're really looking for."

"We're looking for information," Bigelow said. "Who hired you, what kind of an illusion program do they have, stuff like that."

"I'll tell you everything," the man said. "In exchange for my freedom. But you won't believe it unless I demonstrate the box."

"I don't trust this," Paula said. "The box could

be a bomb or something. He'll blow it up and us with it, covering his tracks."

Bigelow knew the man was vicious enough to do that. If he couldn't win, he might see that all of them lost, a suicide bomber.

"So what do we do now?" Bigelow asked the phone. "If we want the information now, we have to trust him, and I don't trust him."

"We doubt he wants to blow himself up with you," the phone said. "Otherwise he would have done it instead of using the knife."

"So you think we can trust him to that extent?" Paula asked. "As long as we keep him handcuffed and tied? And watch him closely?"

"We think so," the phone agreed. "If he can demonstrate the box while in that condition. Otherwise we can't afford to risk a deal."

"All right," Bigelow said more briskly than he felt. "We'll give you that much of a chance. But first, what's your name? Anonymous?"

"Just call me Legion," he said. "In the Bible, when the man was asked about the evil spirits in him, he said 'our name is Legion.'"

Bigelow whistled inwardly. If they had not known this man was trouble, this would have given them the hint. A host of evil spirits! But what could they do? They needed to get information Legion had, and this seemed to be the only feasible way, risky as it was.

Bigelow put the box in Legion's handcuffed hands. "We expect you to cooperate. If you don't, we'll take your box away. Okay?"

"That's fine," Legion said, running his fingers over the surface of the box. "First some background. This device is more advanced."

"More advanced than what?" Paula asked alertly. "Than the eye-test-implanted receivers we have? You have to be specific."

"Right on, cutie," Legion said, eyeing her as if he could see through her clothes. "It needs no implantation. Only brief contact."

"No contact!" Paula snapped, blushing. Then she realized he was teasing her. "You mean with the box? We both just handled it."

"That's right, sweetbuns. You have been zeroed in. So it can send you illusions. There are limitations, but they can be effective."

"We've had some experience with illusions," Bigelow said. "We have learned how to handle them. How is this superior to those?"

"For one thing, it's much easier to zero in, so a large number of people can be set up," Legion said. "Millions, maybe, in days."

"Millions!" Bigelow said. "You couldn't get millions of people into this office within days, even just for one-second touches."

"One second touches," Legion echoed, eyeing Paula's shirt. She crossed her arms defensively. "I like that. But no, not that way."

"Then what way?" Bigelow asked, frowning. He didn't like the way Legion kept making Paula react. "Be specific, as we said."

"We'll produce thousands of boxes and make them widely available. Maybe have a contest: find the hidden switch, win a prize."

"So millions could touch them, unknowingly," Bigelow agreed. "That could do it. But sending individual illusions would be a chore."

"Not individual illusions," Legion said. "The same illusion, sent out to everyone at the same time, wherever they are. Easy to do."

"But people would quickly see through that," Paula protested. "If everybody saw the same rattlesnake, that's obvious illusion."

"Ah, but suppose they saw a trailer truck veer out of its lane and hurtle directly toward them?" Legion smiled. "They'd veer."

"Not if they were in their living rooms," Paula said. "Again, they'd know it had to be illusion, especially if they were warned."

"And how many would be on the road," Bigelow asked. "Maybe one in ten? Many of whom would be stopped at traffic lights."

"Sure," Legion agreed. "Say only one in a

hundred is driving in traffic at that moment. Of one million. That's ten thousand."

Now they saw it. Ten thousand desperate swerves to avoid the trailer truck. Ten thousand likely accidents. How many deaths?

"There would be some chain crashes," Legion said. "As cars behind them plowed into the wreckage. Some fiery explosions."

Paula winced. "The illusions might not be real, but their effects would be real and devastating. Much mischief there, I fear."

"Other illusions, strategically placed and timed, could bring down airplanes, even ships," Legion said. "Mischief indeed."

"Still, after the initial mayhem, folk would be warned, and careful," Bigelow said. "The damage would not be unduly persistent."

"Subsequent illusions would be targeted to take out food and fuel supply lines," Legion said. "There'd be riots soon enough."

"Still, that would not be enough to bring down a great nation like ours," Paula said. "We'd survive and fight back, I'm sure."

"Not if the enemy struck at the height of the crisis," Legion said. "With the military out of food and gasoline. You'd be goners."

"It could be bad," Bigelow agreed. "If the box can really do those mass illusions. Fortunately we have captured your box."

"Well, let's see about that," Legion said. He stroked the box. Suddenly in his place was a crouching tiger. It looked up, growling.

Bigelow was impressed. An illusion with sight and sound, all from the little box. He glanced at Paula, and knew she saw it too.

Then the tiger got up and advanced slowly toward them. "It's not real," Bigelow said. "We can safely stand our ground. I'm sure."

"But suppose Legion is crawling toward us, covered by the tiger?" Paula asked fearfully. "He could grab me and get the key."

The key to the handcuffs. If Legion got hold of her and threatened to kill her unless Bigelow gave him the key, what would he do?

"I think we shouldn't have given him the box," Bigelow said. "But we can separate. If he grabs one of us, the other can bash him."

"You've got his ceramic knife," Paula said. "If he grabs you, use it on him without mercy." She paused. "Which leaves me."

"You take the knife," Bigelow said, pressing it into her hand. "I'll use my fist, maybe." He was bluffing; he didn't want to fight.

"You're so brave," Paula said. "I love you." Then she kissed him and walked quickly across the room. She stood there nervously.

Meanwhile the tiger had stopped just out of reach. Bigelow could guess why: it was illusion, and Legion remained tied on the floor.

Bigelow pondered. He was not brave, but he was desperate. Maybe he should charge across and grab Legion and yank the box from him.

Then the tiger faded out. They looked to the wall where Legion had been. He was not there. "Oh, darn," Paula breathed. "He's gone!"

"He can't be gone," Bigelow said. "He must have crawled to a place of hiding while we were distracted by the tiger. Cunning knave."

"Then we've got to find him before he gets away," Paula said. "He didn't use the door; it never opened. Maybe behind the desk?"

They looked all around the desk. No Legion. But where else was there? "Maybe the bathroom," Bigelow said. "Waiting in ambush."

They went to the bathroom door. It was a unisex facility, for this small office, with one sink, one urinal and one toilet stall.

"I'll go in," Bigelow said. "You stay out here. That way I will be sure that whatever is in there is either illusion, or him."

"You're so brave," she repeated nervously. "I'm terrified. But if I hear anything, I'll come in with the knife ready. I love you."

That was the second time she had said that,

but it helped. If she said it a hundred times, it would help a hundred times. "Thanks."

Bigelow nerved himself and pushed open the bathroom door, ready to strike out. Legion must still be shackled, but still dangerous.

There was nothing. The bathroom was empty. He could see all of it, because one wall was a large mirror. No fugitive. No Legion. Where could the man have gone? If he was not in the office, and not in the bathroom, where was he? Then Bigelow got an idea.

"He made an illusion of the floor and wall without him there!" he exclaimed to himself. "He's still where we left him!" He hoped.

Bigelow pulled open the door, which had swung closed behind him. He took one step forward and paused, appalled. There was Legion! The killer was standing where Paula had been, his hands still shackled, his legs free. He must have untied the nylon cord.

What had he done with Paula? She was nowhere in sight. Somehow Legion had caught her and disposed of her. Now it was just they two.

Blind rage swept Bigelow up. He no longer cared about the danger or his lack of training. He charged Legion, his fists balled. But Legion dodged, and Bigelow's shoulder caught him a glancing blow. He whirled, grabbing the man about the waist, lifting him. Bigelow staggered back into the bathroom door, pushing it open, and through, trying to get a better hold on him. Paula screamed.

Paula screamed? That meant she was alive, and close by. Bigelow shot a glance at the big mirror. And froze. Because he saw—

He saw two Legions grappling each other. Neither Paula nor Bigelow were reflected in the mirror. Which was impossible.

"Bigelow!" Paula said in his ear. "It's us! We're fighting each other! Because the illusion makes us both see Legion instead."

It had to be true. Now he realized that the person he held was not large and muscular, but small and slender. It was Paula.

"I love you too," he said. Then he kissed the rough face of Legion the killer. Appearance be damned! It was definitely her.

"I could do this forever," she said. "But we must catch him before he gets away." She wriggled free. "But we'd better hold hands."

So they would not mistake each other again. He could have bashed her, and she could have stabbed him, because of the illusion. What a deadly ploy it had been! To make each of them think the other was Legion, and make them attack each other, and maybe—

Bigelow banished that thought. Hand in hand they ran out of the bathroom. Now Legion was there, almost to the office door.

"No you don't!" Bigelow cried, tackling him. He wrestled the man down while Paula grabbed the illusion box. They had him.

Deprived of the box, and still manacled, Legion was helpless. He had untied his feet, but that wasn't enough. They retied him.

"We've got him," Bigelow told the phone. "And the box. Now get your people over here to pick up both. We have what you need."

"Congratulations," the phone said. "Our people are already on the way. You have saved the situation. You are heroes."

Bigelow and Paula exchanged a glance. They knew they had not only salvaged the office, they had enabled the Project folk to win. Because with their prisoner and the illusion box, they would soon have all the information they needed to stop the enemy attack.

But somehow right now all they cared about was each other. The rest could wait its turn. However long it might take. They were heroes for the hour. Even if their lives became dull again, Bigelow and Paula knew they would be happy together.

"DULL STREET INCIDENT"

This commences the fourth Tweet story, titled "Dull Street Incident." It is mainstream, not Fantasy, but maybe has its points. The characters are all nameless, to protect the guilty from possible retaliation, even though they did nothing wrong, maybe.

A newspaper investigative reporter was running low on scandals and needed something local and spicy. He had a nose for news. He got wind of something that happened on Dull Street, where nothing interesting ever occurred. Was that an oxymoron? He would damn well find out. He checked Dull Street on the city map. It was only three blocks long with no intersections. It was in a boring medium-scale residential neighborhood: single story houses, unkempt yards, flaking paint, tattered fences. Most residents worked in the nearby industrial complex, drawing salaries that were losing the race against inflation. Their children attended the local lower-tier schools, and few went on to become even moderately successful or educated. There was essentially nothing to do on Dull Street: no movie theater, no dance hall, no skating rink, no shopping mall. There was no sign of any fire or car wreck or other interesting disaster. Nothing had changed in years on Dull Street. There were only two things of even remotely possible interest nearby: the county prison and the city dump. No help there.

But maybe there was a lead. The reporter checked the prison records, and learned that recently a prison work group had been there. They had gone the length of the street hacking out weeds, clearing discarded junk, scrubbing off the sidewalks, erasing graffiti. In one day they had made Dull Street look slightly less unkempt, then gone on to the next street. It was strictly routine.

Could a prisoner have slipped away, robbed a house, and rejoined the crew, nobody else the wiser? Most houses were empty by day. But there was no report of any robbery there that day. The work crew prisoners were rough, tough, brutal men, but none had strayed. Of course not all crimes got reported. The theft might not even have been discovered. But then, what was the source of the rumor?

The reporter researched the records and got the names of all the members of that day's prison work crew. He interviewed them all. The crew leader was a small man, a would-be promoter who had fallen on recessionary times and taken what work he could get. The prisoners were all big, strong, tough men of several races, in for crimes ranging from, yes, theft to reckless violence. It seemed unlikely that such a small, inexperienced guard could maintain order among brutally experienced prisoners.

In fact, the situation smelled of a prison authority that wanted to be rid of a seeming weakling, giving him rope to hang himself. So they had sent him out on a work crew with the worst of the worst, anticipating his loss of control and a firing-caliber foul-up. But there had been no trouble. In fact the rough prisoners seemed to respect this weakling guard. They had worked well for him. There had been no complaints from the residents of Dull Street. In fact they appreciated the good job the crew had done.

The reporter questioned every prisoner on that crew, trying to provoke some telltale reaction. There was none. Yet they were lying. The reporter had an innate sense, an invaluable aid to his business of sniffing out scandal. He could almost literally smell a lie. And they all were lying. They said the day had been completely routine. They had cleaned up Dull Street and moved on. Untrue.

What were they hiding? It must be big, to evoke so determined a cover-up. Why were none of the prisoners willing to squeal? The reporter was supremely frustrated. He knew there was something, but he could not get at it. He returned to Dull Street. He walked up and down the length of it, finding only a neatly cleaned up neighborhood. The crew had done its job well.

Then a boy rode up on a skateboard, enjoying the cleared sidewalk. He looked at the reporter. "I know what happened."

Was this a joke? "What?" the reporter asked.

"I'll tell if we make a deal."

"What deal?"

"I want a newspaper tour."

"For what?"

"For telling you what happened," the boy said.

The reporter didn't trust this. "What happened where? When? To whom?"

"What happened here on Dull Street that day the prisoner work crew came by. I sneak read my big sister's diary. I know it all."

This seemed authentic. "Are you free now?" the reporter asked.

"Sure."

"Then tell me while we tour the newspaper."

"Okay!"

The reporter took the boy to the newspaper and showed him everything from the front offices to the printing press. They talked. Now at last the reporter learned about the Dull Street Incident that no one else would talk about. His feelings were mixed. He questioned the boy, filling in what details he could. There were gaps, but in due course he had enough of it to be satisfied. The reporter was able to interpolate likely aspects the boy was missing, to complete the story. To grasp the delicate nuances.

The prison guard knew he had been sent out on a virtual suicide mission. The men were surly and eager for trouble. Worse, the prisoners knew they had him at their mercy. They had little to lose, while he needed this job. Any little incident...

Still, if they got him fired, he would be replaced by a more experienced and cynical guard. A tougher one. They knew that too. So it behooved them to keep it nice, if their underlying viciousness didn't get the better of them. But would they? Doubtful.

It started calmly enough. The truck dropped them off at the end of Dull Street: a dozen big rough men. One small guard.

They took the tools and started in, knowing what to do. All the guard had to do was stay out of their way. If they let him. They hacked the weeds, using the swinging tool that could as readily slice through an ankle. They chopped out fallen branches. They clipped out matted vines, shoveled out dirt, made piles of rocks and discarded junk. Slowly they advanced along the street.

But the guard knew they were just biding their time, looking for their opportunity to mess up spectacularly, blaming him for it.

Then he saw something. Two rather pretty teen girls were crying at the edge of a yard, trying unsuccessfully to console each other.

Now he voiced his first direct command. "At ease." The men paused, having been given leave to rest a moment. They looked around.

The guard approached the girls. "Excuse me, young women," he said. "We are a prison work detail, doing our job. Is there a problem?"

The two girls were glad to share. "We made a deal to clean up a back yard today, to earn money for the school dance tonight. But—"

"Yes?" he asked sympathetically.

"But look at it," the cute little blonde said. "It's such a mess we'll never get it done in time!"

"And just trying it will get us all sweaty and scratched and dirty, ruining us for the dance anyway," the buxom brunette concluded.

"We hadn't seen it before we got here," the blonde said. "We thought it would be easy. Just some grass to mow, weeds to pull."

"We were fools," the brunette said. "We should have checked it out before making the deal. Now we're stuck. Utterly screwed."

An idea burst like a bright light. "Ladies, perhaps we can solve your problem. But there is a price."

"Price?" the blonde asked.

"Let me explain," the guard said. "You don't have to do it if you don't want to and I appreciate why you might not want to." Then he explained.

The girls considered, consulted, and smiled. "We can do that," the brunette said. "Provided no one tells."

"No one will tell," the guard promised. Then he returned to the prisoners. "Men," he said quietly. "Trust me for an hour." They looked at him, committing to nothing. "We are going to make a small detour," he continued. "We will see nothing."

The big rough prisoners considered. What did this weakling guard have in mind? Then the biggest brute spoke. "One hour."

"Follow me," the guard said. He led the way into the yard the girls needed to clean up. "Police the area. You know how." They shrugged and went to work with their assorted tools. What was impossible for the girls was routine for them.

Meanwhile the two girls fetched clothing and

supplies from their car. They went to an outdoor shower nestled behind the house. They laid out their things. Then they began to strip. "We see nothing," the guard murmured. "Keep working." Surprised, the men did. The work crew prisoners were coming to understand the deal the guard had made. All they had to do was keep working, and looking.

The girls stripped nude, put on shower caps, and stepped into the shower. "Eeeek!" they screamed as the cold water hit them. They washed each other off, their shapely young bodies bouncing freely. They pretended the watching prisoners did not exist.

The men continued working, efficiently cleaning up the yard. But they saw everything, pretending they saw nothing. What a deal!

The girls finished their shower, splendidly shook themselves off, and toweled each other dry. Then they started dressing. They put on their panties. The brunette put on her bra, filling it well, fastening it in front. The blonde's bra hooked in back.

"Pause," the guard murmured. The men stopped working and just looked. The girls, it seemed, did not see them at all.

The blonde glanced at the guard, and faintly nodded. Then she struggled to hook her bra behind her, but kept missing the connection.

The guard looked at the biggest prisoner, nodding to the girl. "Tie that loose vine."

Amazed, the prisoner just stood there. "Now."

The prisoner dropped weed cutter and gloves and walked to the blonde, who remained facing away from him, struggling with her bra. He took the two ends of the bra straps, brought them together, and hooked them. The loose vine had been tied. He stepped back.

The girl turned around. Wordlessly she stepped forward, kissed the prisoner on the cheek, and turned quickly away, blushing.

"Resume," the guard said. The prisoners resumed their work, including the biggest, toughest one, who seemed to be in a daze. By the time the girls completed their dressing and primping, the men had finished cleaning up the yard. Both jobs looked very good.

"Move out," the guard said. "Remember, we saw nothing. We just did our dull routine job." The prison crew moved out.

"Maybe we can do it again sometime," the blonde said to the brunette, loud enough to be heard. "Though we saw nothing."

"Maybe we can," the brunette agreed. "This yard looks just perfect!" The two of them stood there admiring the yard.

The prisoners smiled as they returned to the street and resumed their work there. They knew what looked perfect. No one spoke of the incident on Dull Street, but thereafter the new guard had no trouble with the men. They understood each other. There had been no open deal. No one had seen anything. Even the kiss had not been stolen, but given as appreciation.

The reporter pondered the matter. He realized that nothing could be gained by blowing this whistle. A guard might be fired. Prisoners might be restricted. Two girls might be perpetually grounded. And for what? Nothing had happened, really, had it?

All he could do, maybe, was write it up as fiction, with a far-away setting. An incident that never happened. Who would believe it?

"FORBIDDEN FRUIT"

This commences Tweet Story #5, titled "Forbidden Fruit."

Edith was a 50 year old divorcee, reasonably set financially, but unsatisfied. She had lost her husband to a woman half her age. She knew that was the way men were, hopelessly superficial, always with eyes on youth instead of maturity. But still it irked her.

She had moved to this apartment complex, but had not yet gotten acquainted with the other inhabitants, not even those on her floor. The prior occupant of this suite had cleared out all her things, but overlooked one: an odd fruit in a drawer of the refrigerator. Edith would have returned it to her, but the woman had departed for parts unknown. Uncertain what to do with it, she let it be.

Until one day she discovered that the fruit was sprouting. It was roughly cubical, and the sprout was square in cross section. Curious, she took the fruit out and studied it more closely. It was striped with red and green bands and the growing stem was gray.

She put it in a pot with good moist soil, by a window with morning sunlight, and it grew rapidly. The leaves were square and blue. Edith tried to research the fruit and plant, but could find nothing even close. It seemed to be one of a quite unusual kind.

In a week it was about two feet tall and well filled out with branches and leaves. She was amazed by the velocity of its growth. Then it flowered, and that was another surprise. The blooms were cubic and black. She waited for the first one to open. It didn't. It just sat there, a glossy cube about an inch on a side, hiding whatever was inside. What was it waiting for? An invitation?

There was no smell, no indication. It was a locked locket, secret. Finally Edith extended a forefinger cautiously and touched it. Then the flower opened explosively, releasing a small cloud of purple vapor. Edith accidentally breathed it. And paused, amazed.

Because suddenly she had a phenomenal new awareness. She could see around corners. She could hear the faint thoughts of neighbors. Her feet lifted from the floor. She could float and fly! She could move objects merely by looking at them and willing the motion. She tried it with a heavy couch. It rose an inch, moved, and settled down a little to the side. She had telepathy and telekinesis!

Did she really? She went to the couch and checked. It was definitely in a new place; she saw the old marks of its feet on the floor. Maybe these were psionic powers, super science or magnetism or whatnot. Mind control of physical things. But it seemed like magic.

Or was she hallucinating? That seemed far more likely. She needed a more objective judgment. But there was no one else to ask. So she continued to experiment. She became invisible, including her clothing. She walked through a wall, ghost-like. What next?

Then she got a wicked idea. She made herself half her age. Suddenly her dress was loose about her waist and tight about her chest. Edith looked in the large bathroom mirror. Then she stripped naked and looked again. She was definitely a healthy 25 year old woman. She turned in place, admiring her well-formed breasts and her firm shapely buttocks and her nicely fleshed thighs. Wow! Perfection!

Unless it was just her foolish imagination. She just had to have the input of another person, who had not breathed the purple vapor. Well, why not?

She walked through the door without opening it and down the hall to the apartment of her handsome young neighbor.

The plaque on the door said KENT. She knocked. In a moment the door opened. Kent stood there, staring without speaking.

Then Edith realized that she had not dressed again, after the mirror. She was flashing him with a perfect nude 25 year old woman.

Well, in for a nickel, in for a dime. "Hello," she said. "I think I need a friend."

"I didn't know Edith had a daughter!" he said.

Oops! He recognized the resemblance. Her face had not changed as much as her body. "I'm not exactly that," she said cautiously. Meanwhile she was thrilled to verify that he did see her, and saw her as young not middle aged, and that they could interact. So the magic was real; it was not her personal hallucination. Not imagination. He had just alleviated her most worrisome doubt.

"Oh, her niece?" he asked. Edith grasped at that. "Yes. I'm—Eden. Visiting for a few days." Because he'd never believe the truth.

"But you're naked!"

Edith thought fast. "Yes. That's why I need help. I was going to take a shower, but stepped out the wrong door." Would he buy that story?

"And got stranded without the key," he said.

He was accepting it! "Yes. It's awkward. Could I come in?"

"Of course," he said. He opened the door wide, and she stepped into his apartment. "Let me get you a robe." He hurried off.

Edith breathed a silent sigh of relief. Not only was she verifying the reality of the magic, she was learning Kent was a nice guy.

He returned in a moment with a somewhat scruffy bathrobe. "Sorry—this is all I've got."

"It's fine," she said, putting it on.

"Can I get you something to drink?" He paused, embarrassed. "Like water?"

Edith did a quick assessment. Was he coming on to her? More important: was she interested? She knew what healthy 25 year old women did. They captured the interest and passion of men. Now she was one of those sirens. Why shouldn't she enjoy the perquisites? Also, she was curious about the limits of this conversion. Could this body perform the way it promised?

There was one way to find out. "Do you have wine?" That was a fairly open invitation.

Kent jumped to oblige. He fetched two glasses and a bottle of cheap wine: what he could afford. He poured it out and proffered one.

She took it. "Thank you," she said, smiling fetchingly. "You are most hospitable." And realized that she was speaking her real age. A young woman would be far less formal. "I mean, cheers." She lifted her glass to him, then sipped. He matched her, mesmerized.

She realized that even though he was young and handsome, he probably did not get many really nice dates, because he wasn't rich. She could be a really nice date. She wasn't rich either, but she was comfortable. What she lacked was adventure and romance. And here it was. She had but to grasp it. If it didn't work out, what had she lost? Something she had not thought to have anyway.

"Uh, are you single?" he asked. He was eager yet hesitant, which meant she could control this relationship. She liked that also.

"I am single," she agreed. "But maybe not exactly what I may appear to be." She didn't want to lie outright, so was purposely vague.

"You look like the woman of my dreams."

Oh, great! She smiled, letting the bathrobe fall open slightly. She saw his pupils dilate. Oh, it was fun being 25! Having the wherewithal to fascinate a man in an instant. What phenomenal power! She took a deep breath.

Kent seemed about to faint. He licked his lips, his gaze locked. It was time. "Kiss me," she said, standing, not closing the robe.

He didn't hesitate. Ah the impetuosity of

youth! He enfolded her and kissed her. The kiss was amateur but nevertheless electrifying. Because his unfeigned ardor was a potent turn-on for her too. In her marriage sex had become routine, then unsatisfying, then rare. She knew exactly how to do it, but the excitement had dissipated. Yet this seduction, with Kent, was daring, new, and exciting.

After a brief eternity it ended. He drew back a bit and gazed into her eyes. "Oh, Eden, I don't know you, but I think I love you."

She laughed. "If that's what you tell all the girls you date, it's effective." She was pretty sure it wasn't a line; he was serious.

"You're just so great!" He took a breath. "I can't help myself. I've got to have more of you, Eden. Tell me to quit and I will."

Edith knew she should tell him the truth, now, before they went further. But either he would not believe her, so what was the point? Or he would believe her, and be turned off, and she would lose her chance to put this marvelous body through its ultimate paces. So she was silent. After all, "Eden" was supposed to be here only for a few days. She could disappear without awkward complications.

Kent kissed her again, and again it was electric. This young body of hers reacted much more powerfully to stimuli than her own did. Soon they were both naked on his unmade bed, and he was all over her, kissing all over. She did not protest. In fact she cooperated.

Then he paused. "Last chance, Eden. Tell me to leave off."

"No," she whispered.

"Is that no don't do it?"

"No."

"You sure?"

"Yes."

Then they were in the throes of it, and it was every bit as wonderful as she had dared to hope. This body definitely was for real.

"Now I know I love you," he said as they lay beside each other on the bed. "You really ring my bell, Eden."

She squeezed his hand. "I'm a belle," she agreed. "I love you too, in my fashion. But—" Could she actually tell him the truth now? If not now, when?

Then she became aware of something else, awful. The magic was fading! Like Cinderella, she had to get out of here immediately. "But I must go," she said, scrambling to her feet. "You're perfect, it's been great, but I've got to get to the—the bathroom now."

"But you can't get in without your key," he protested. "You can use mine."

But she was already barging out into the hall, desperate. She ran to her door while he was still scrambling into his clothes. Then his words sank in:

she couldn't get in to her apartment. She was about to become a middle aged woman, naked in the hall. She had not escaped embarrassing discovery; she had made it worse.

Then she suffered a flash of near genius. With the last of her dissipating magic she conjured her clothing from the bathroom floor. Her key was in her dress. Now she could open the door, get inside, and collapse in relieved reversion. But there was a problem.

In her haste she had gotten details of the conjuration wrong. She had her clothing, and her key, but the devil lay in those details. Her dress was on backward. Under it her panties were wrapped around her chest and her bra was supporting her buttocks. Ouch!

Then Kent barreled out of his apartment, buttoning his shirt. Edith was still fumbling for her key. It was too late to escape.

She got another flash. She faced Kent. "Have you seen my niece?" she asked him. "She disappeared, and I can't find her anywhere."

"I—I—" he said, flustered.

"She's so impulsive!" Edith said. "She must have wandered away, yet her clothing remains here."

"I—I may have seen her," he stammered. "But she left. I—I really want to see her again."

Edith seized the initiative. "And?"

"And we kissed," he said. "I think I love her."

"You kissed her?" she demanded. "You say you love her? You don't even know her!"

"It's crazy, I know. But she's my dream woman. I've got to find her. Please, if you have any idea—" He broke off, observing her. "What happened to you, Ms. Edith? You look as if you were mugged. Your clothing is all fouled up. Were you—were you raped?"

"No, of course not. I just—" But how could she ever explain? She knew she was a frightful sight.

"This is weird," Kent said. "First Eden runs this way, and now here you are, all messed up. Did you collide with her?"

"Something like that, maybe," she said. He was starting to catch on. He wasn't stupid. Ordinarily she would have liked that too. "Kent, I think we must seriously talk."

"You bet," he agreed grimly. "Your place or mine?"

That made her pause. His place had the open bed. Her place had the magic plant. "My place," she decided. "Just give me a moment to put myself in order."

In due course they were seated in her petite living room. "It began with the strange fruit," she said. "I found it in the refrigerator, and when it sprouted I planted it out of curiosity."

"Forbidden fruit," he said.

"Yes, perhaps. It grew rapidly and flowered,

and when I sniffed a bloom, it gave me magic for a while."

"Magic?"

"This is where it becomes difficult to believe," she said. "Suddenly I could fly, and move objects with my mind, and—"

"And turn twenty five?"

"Yes. But I feared it was just my imagination, so I walked through the door and looked you up. To verify."

"Eden is you?"

"Yes. I didn't like deceiving you; I just wanted to be sure that I really was young again. Then I got carried away."

"So did I," Kent said. "Eden was such a lovely creature, and somehow she knew how to push my buttons. I still think I love her."

"Until this moment," Edith said. "Now you know she's not real."

He shook his head. "She *is* real. Just not in the way I thought."

"But she has no separate identity. She's just me as I wish I could be." She sighed. "If I could have gotten away cleanly I'd have—"

"You'd have what?" he asked.

"I'd have sniffed the next bloom tomorrow and visited you again as Eden. I really enjoyed our tryst." There. She had said it. How would he react?

"As Eden," he echoed.

"I'm sorry. I didn't mean to be a cougar. I acted impulsively."

"As Eden," he repeated.

"Yes," she said. "I'm just so hungry for meaningful interaction, especially of the romantic variety."

"Even the sex?"

"Especially the sex. That young body is *alive*. I enjoyed it as much as you did, I'm sure. I would have continued."

He was silent. How was he reacting? She decided to go for broke. "And I would still do it, if you accede. Tell me to quit."

Finally he spoke. "I'll be blunt. It's Eden I want, not a cougar. You will do for a friend, not a lover. That may be shallow of me. But it's the way I am."

"But you can't have Eden without knowing that mentally she's a middle aged woman. Can you stand that?"

"If you can handle my wanting your young body, I can handle your mature mind."

"I'll be darned," she said. "You really don't care what's in a woman's head as long as her body looks good?"

"Did you care what was in my head as long as my body was yours?"

"Touché!" They both laughed.

"But it's not quite as simple as that," he continued. "Eden is you, and my knowing that doesn't make her suddenly less attractive. What I knew of her was you. I fell in love with that aspect of you. Without you she would be less."

"I'll be darned," Edith repeated. "Well, come here tomorrow and watch me change. Then do me if you still want to. I'm willing."

"You're on! I'm really curious about that plant, now, too."

"Well, come see it now." She took him into the kitchen where it was.

"It's an odd one," Kent said. "It must be from an alien world."

"Maybe so," she agreed. "But how did it get in my refrigerator?"

"Somebody must have put it there."

"But where did she get it?"

"No, I mean someone else. Put it there for you to find. To plant."

"Put there for me to find," she repeated, awed. "Maybe that makes more sense. But why would anyone waste such a treasure on me?"

"Maybe he has dozens of them, so they're cheap, for him." He paused to look at her. "Maybe he wants artificial young women."

Edith mulled that over, intrigued. "Who would do anything he wanted, just to be young again. A stable of eager captive mistresses."

"It's the way men think," Kent said.

"But suppose a man rented the apartment?" she asked.

"Well, some men like men," he said.

She shook her head. "There are many ways to buy men and women, far simpler than this. It must be something else."

"I suppose so. But there must be a price. You might not like that price, when the fruitier comes."

She shuddered. "That scares me."

"I saw a horror movie once where these weird plants sort of ate their owners."

"But those plants didn't give them magic," she said.

"So it's something else," Kent said. "But I'd be wary. Really wary."

"Maybe I should throw it out."

He winced. "And I'd lose Eden."

"So it seems we're already hooked," she said. "I want youth, and you want me young."

"Hooked," he said thoughtfully. "Could—?"

"Could the fruit be bait?" she completed his sentence. "The fisherman casts it out on the water and waits for the fish to bite?"

"I think it could," he said.

"But what could anyone with fantastic magic like this want with a nobody like me?" she asked.

"That is the question," Kent said. "No offense."

"None taken. I think we'd better answer it. What is worth more than magic?"

That stumped them both. "It can't be anything bought with money, because with magic you could conjure barrels of gold," he said.

"Well, let's adjourn until the morrow," she suggested. "Come in early afternoon."

"Right. I job-hunt in the morning." He departed.

Edith gazed at the plant. "I wonder whether you are not more trouble than you're worth," she mused. "Yet that magic is tempting."

She looked at the couch. It was back in its original place. That made her pause. She was sure it had been moved. It had reverted? But her interaction with Kent had been real. They had had phenomenal sex, and a most interesting dialogue. That had not reverted.

Edith shook her head. It was too much to untangle at the moment. They could tackle such questions tomorrow. Now she wanted to relax. But one image continued to play through her mind as she did her evening chores and turned in. A pretty lure floating on water.

Kent arrived on schedule next afternoon. "You're just in time," Edith said. "The second bloom is ready. Do you wish to share it?"

"No. Not this time," he said. "It's not that I don't trust you, but that I don't trust it. I need to know more about it first."

"Fair enough. You can be the observer. Maybe you will see things I don't." She leaned carefully toward the bloom, then touched it. It exploded, and its purple vapor surrounded her head. This time she breathed deeply, deliberately, taking it in. She felt dizzy.

Then her head cleared. She looked at Kent. "See anything untoward?"

"Just a puff of dissipating vapor. You're unchanged."

"We'll see." She willed herself young again, and felt the immediate shifting of her proportions. Then she threw off the robe. She was nude beneath it, with no clothing or underwear. She had come prepared this time. She turned slowly around before him.

"Oh, my!" Kent said. "Welcome back, Eden!"

"You saw me change," she reminded him. "You know I'm the same woman. Still interested?"

"Yes!" he exclaimed. "I thought it might turn me off, but I've come to terms with it and like you just the way you are now."

"Then I am yours." She went to him and kissed him. She had thought it would be OK, but there was always that nagging doubt.

He enfolded her, kissing her avidly, his hands

running over her body. Then they adjourned to her bedroom for the grand finale. She loved all of it. This time there was more than one siege, as she guided him to a second effort, teaching him what worked best.

Then it was time to practice magic. She showed him how she could become invisible, float, fly, conjure, and walk through walls.

"Awesome," he said. "Can you read my mind?"

She did. "You're picturing me nude," she said. "Which is pointless, because I *am* nude."

"Yes, but can you tell what I want to do with you?"

"Better than that. I can show you." She projected a picture of him kissing her.

"And now?" The mental picture showed her turning away. He goosed her. She swung around and slapped his face. All in the image.

They laughed. "You can read my mind, all right," he said. "Not that there's anything very subtle about it."

"Well, you're a man." They laughed again, understanding each other perfectly.

Then they got serious about magic. "How many things can you do at once?"

"Most of them, I think," she said. She floated through a wall then conjured a pile of golden coins while aloft and made them dance.

"And you remain young," he said. "You don't

have to quit one thing to do another. It's cumulative."

"It's cumulative," she agreed. "But there is one thing," she said, and told him about how she had moved the couch, but it had reverted. "Yet our tryst did not."

Kent pondered that. "Our tryst, as you put it, left no physical trace. It exists only in our memories. But the couch was physical."

"It was physical," she agreed. "Maybe that's the limit: I can do things magically, but they don't stay done. Only their memories."

"And we can test it now," he said. "Move the couch again." She focused, and the couch lifted a foot high, and moved two feet right.

It slowly settled in the new location. Kent touched it, verifying that its position had changed. "But wait till the magic ends."

"That should be within an hour, based on yesterday's experience."

"Then let's make out again before it fades."

"A one track mind."

"You bet. You object?"

"Not at all." They adjourned to the bedroom again. By the time they were done, she felt the fading.

This time she covered up but did not flee. They checked the couch. It was back in place. Also, the piled gold coins were gone.

"So now we know about reversion," Kent said.

"Magic is temporary, unfortunately. Yet I wonder whether that can be the whole story."

"What are you thinking of?" she asked.

"Well, suppose you conjure a coin, and use it to get a chocolate candy bar from a machine."

"I love chocolate. I'd eat it." She paused. "Oh. You meant what would happen when the magic faded? Would it still be there?"

"Exactly. Can we use magic to accomplish something, and have the accomplishment remain after the magic dissipates? Or not?"

She nodded. "The couch reverted. The gold coins evaporated. But can an action by us really be undone? I find that hard to believe."

"So do I. But I think we had better check. Because if actions endure, we could conjure gold and buy a house, and keep the house."

"Instant wealth," she agreed. "From temporary money. That seems like a loophole."

"So tomorrow I'll sniff the flower, and try it."

"Wonderful! I'll be the objective party." Then she thought of something. "But I won't become Eden. Unless you can change me."

"That's another thing," he said. "Can a person with magic change a person without magic? That would be almost scary power."

"Scary," she agreed. "But intriguing. Promise not to change me into a turkey."

"I promise. I wouldn't care for sex with a turkey."

Kent departed, and Edith relaxed. She liked him, liked him a lot. He had navigated the hurdle of seeing her change, and was being really helpful with the exploration of the magic, thinking of things she didn't. She felt more confident with his participation. But that business of the fruit set out for her to find—a planted plant—made her nervous. When would the bill for this fun come due?

Next afternoon Kent came for the third flower's blooming. This time he was the one who touched it and inhaled the purple vapor.

Edith saw him stand unsteadily for a moment, reorienting. Then he regained control. He looked at her. "I can do magic!" he said.

"Yes," she agreed. "Try some routine tricks first, like floating or looking through walls, to be sure you have it pat."

He nodded. Kent floated up to the ceiling, then flew around the room without wings. He landed and conjured several silver coins. "Wow!"

"Exhilarating, isn't it," she said. "You should be able to do just about anything you can think of, just by willing it to happen."

"Yeah. It's great." He peered at the wall, and she knew he was looking through it. "Oh, my! I see Ms. Tompkins taking a shower."

"Magic is great for voyeurism," Edith agreed, unconcerned.

"Yeah. Too bad she's not thinner and younger." He looked away, frowning.

"That's the problem with the average woman. Not pretty. Now try me," Edith said. Her heart was suddenly pounding. Would this work?

Kent focused on her. Nothing happened. "You're too complicated," he said. "I can't get the feel of you. I mean, the living tissue."

"Maybe that makes sense," she said. "We're not doctors or surgeons. Messing with other folks' living bodies could be disastrous."

"Maybe I can do it by illusion." He focused again. Edith felt nothing, but her dress changed, making her look voluptuous. Well now.

"You look great," he said. "Just like Eden."

"But underneath the illusion I'm unchanged," she said. "Can you make it tactile too?"

"Maybe." More focusing. She still felt no different.

"There," he said. "May I—touch you? Where it counts? I know you're not Eden."

"Touch me," she agreed, mightily intrigued. Could illusion really make her seem like Eden when she wasn't? And if so—

He approached her and took her in his arms. "You look like her, you feel like her." He hesitated, so she kissed him on the mouth.

"And you kiss like her," he said. "May I—?"

"Of course." She stood still as he squeezed her bottom, then her breasts. How far?

He hesitated. "You're her. But I know it's just illusion. I mean, you *are* her, but—"

"But I'm old," she finished. "Not the same."

"Not the same," he agreed. "I'm sorry." Which absolved her of the decision whether to go all the way, this way. She was relieved.

"I'm just not into older women." He was embarrassed.

"Kent, I understand," she said." Tomorrow I'll be Eden. She's into you."

"Yeah. Thanks. Now let's try that chocolate bar experiment."

Edith was glad to agree. "Conjure some quarters." And they appeared.

They went out and down the hall where there was a cluster of vending machines. Edith fed one of the conjured coins into one. A chocolate bar dropped down. So far it was working. They returned to her apartment, divided the bar, and ate it. It was delicious.

"Now we wait," she said. "We have about half an hour to kill."

"So what do we do to pass the time?"

"Try doubling your own age."

Immediately he was a portly man of close to

fifty, with his belly popping the buttons of his shirt. "Ugh! I don't like this age."

Edith laughed. "You will inevitably get there in time. Better take better care of yourself in the interim. Eat less chocolate."

"I'd better." He reverted to his regular age, and his clothing fit again, with buttons still missing. "I won't do that again."

"Youth is surely better," she said. "Too bad, as they say, that it is wasted on the young."

"Yes. I'd like to stay young forever."

"So what about tomorrow?" she asked.

"Both inhale?"

"Sure," he said. "But we'd better work out our agenda so we don't waste magic."

"I think we've tried just about everything," he said. "What else is there?"

"Finding out who sent the fruit, and why," she said.

"You're right. But how? Ask a magic mirror?"

"Maybe that would work," she said seriously. "Or maybe summon a captive demon."

"With a pentagram and all," he agreed. "Three days ago that would have seemed like a joke."

"No joke," she agreed. "Dangerous."

"Demons are dangerous," he agreed. "Oh, Edith, do we really want to do this? I'm afraid we could wind up in a literal Hell."

She considered that. "I'm afraid that we are already committed, unless we throw away the plant and never touch magic again."

"I've had just three days experience with magic," he said. "It's addictive. I want more of it, not less. Even if Hell threatens."

"So you'd rather summon the demon?" she asked.

"It's really your decision, because it's your plant. But yes, I think I'd rather."

"Then let's do it, tomorrow," she said. "Maybe the demon will be able to answer all our questions."

"Yes. But at what price?"

"Maybe our souls," she said, shuddering. "That's what really frightens me."

"Me too," he agreed. "Let's ponder overnight."

Edith opened her mouth to agree. And paused. There was a faint shimmer, and the illusion about her faded. She was also hungry.

"The magic ended," Kent said. "I just felt that chocolate leave my stomach. So now we have that answer: it's temporary."

"Actions can indeed be undone," she agreed. "Unless it was always illusion, and we never actually ate that chocolate bar."

"Dammit, the sex was real," he protested. "Our experiments were real. I'm sure of it."

"I'm not," she said. "Maybe we imagined it."

"I can't believe that. We both remember it, don't we, when only one of us had the magic."

"Here's a thought experiment," she said. "Suppose Eden was a virgin. She had sex with you during the magic, so was no longer a virgin. But then she reverted."

"So?"

"So is her hymen restored, making her a virgin again?"

"No, of course not."

"But the candy bar was restored, after being eaten."

"Oh shoot!" he said. "If candy can be un-eaten, then maybe sex can be undone too. The hymen's physical, like the gold. Damn."

"But wouldn't it be simpler for all of it to be illusion?" she asked. "So we only remember it without ever actually doing it."

He nodded reluctantly. "A false memory, maybe, or a real memory of an imagined happening. That is more credible. I hate that."

"Why? Isn't our memory of it good, regardless whether we actually did it? What difference does it make?"

He looked at her, pained. "Do you believe that?" he asked.

"I'm not sure," she said.

"But then maybe Eden never even existed. Just

the memory of her."

"With my illusion about my own body being stronger than your artificial illusion about my body," she said. "Because it's mine."

Kent shook his head. "I've got to believe that Eden is real. I love her!"

Edith sighed. "So do I. Your illusion did not change me. But when I became Eden, I truly was different. I was young, vigorous, and passionate. Yours was illusion; mine was real."

"Yes!" he agreed. "You experienced both. You know the difference."

"I know the difference," she agreed. "It was definitely real."

"Which means that reversion does occur, physically, but our memories are real. Memories don't revert."

"They don't," she agreed.

"And we truly had sex." That was evidently important to him.

"We did," she said. And realized that it was important to her too.

"And Eden exists." Ah; there was the key. He had to believe that his young lover was not all in their imagination.

"She exists."

"Tomorrow we'll both sniff the magic," he said. "And Eden and I will make love. Then we'll summon the demon."

"Yes," she agreed. Then she thought of something else. "When you used illusion to make me look like Eden, I was unchanged but willing to go along."

"Yes, I understood that," he said. "I think that was part of my turnoff: I knew you weren't really into it the way Eden was."

"Suppose I had been into it?" she asked. "Unchanged, but wanting your passion? Turned on. Would you have wanted to do it then?"

He thought about that. "I like your mature mind, and Eden's great body and desire. The illusion made the body. So I guess yes."

"Next question: could you project your desire to me, the way I sent you mental pictures, so that I am turned on?"

"Maybe I could."

"That may be another thing to try, when we care to," she said. "To ascertain the limits of the magic. Meanwhile, Eden is fine."

"Eden is fine," he agreed. "I'd rather have her, no offense."

"None at all. I merely want to know what is possible. Just in case."

He looked at her. "I like the way your mind works. I am glad to have you for a friend. When I'm with Eden, I'm blinded by desire."

"When I am Eden, my hormones tend to override my mind. That's fine, when I'm with you. But for rational thought, Edith is better."

"So maybe tomorrow, after we make love," he said thoughtfully, "Eden should revert to Edith before we summon the demon."

"Yes."

That night Edith continued to think about summoning a demon. They agreed that demons were dangerous. It was not too late to stop. Yet her regular life was dull and unfulfilled. She enjoyed the magic and the affair with Kent. Did she want to give those up? No. The danger was a significant part of the fun. If she didn't follow up on this, when or how would she ever get an interesting life? She preferred to gamble. Even if she should wind up in Hell for it. At least Hell should be interesting. What more could she ask? But she would give Kent one more chance to back out. She could do this alone if she had to, though she'd much prefer it with him. Nervously satisfied with her chosen course, she slept. Tomorrow might be very good or very bad. Either way, it should be exciting.

Kent came early next afternoon. "I've been having second and third thoughts," he said. "I don't have much to lose here. But you—"

"I'm middle aged and dull," she said. "I can give it up. You're the one with youth and a future. So if you want to quit, you may."

"I can't find work, and my unemployment is running out. This magic represents my hope for something better. So I'm definitely in."

"So am I," she said. "But there's one other thing. Maybe one of us should remain objective, not under the spell of the magic."

"I hadn't thought of that. You're right. The flower mist enables us to do magic; how else is it affecting us? We just don't know."

"You had better be the objective one," she said.

"And let you take the risk?"

"And let me be Eden."

"Oh, yes," he agreed instantly.

They went to the flower. Edith saw that there were just three more blooms, one mature, two still developing. Six flowers in all.

"I think we'll have two more days to do whatever we're going to do," she said. "Then it will be over."

"Over," he agreed sadly.

She leaned close and touched the flower. It detonated, and she breathed the mist. Then immediately she became Eden, and faced him.

He took her in his arms. "This is what I most truly want," he said. "All else is dross." They kissed, and went to the bedroom. Eden was vitally alive and passionate, but Edith realized that she herself was similarly motivated. She loved being luscious. She wanted to be Eden forever. If there were any way, any way at all, even if Hell was the penalty, she desperately wanted it.

"I would go to Hell to be with you," Kent said, echoing her thought. "I mean that literally. I love you, Eden."

"I feel the same."

Mutually sated, they dressed and Edith reverted to herself, as they had agreed. She did feel more objective, less emotional.

Kent shook his head, bemused. "I love Eden, but right now I'd rather be with you. You have a mature judgment."

"Thank you."

Then they got to work. Kent took a piece of chalk and drew a five pointed star on the floor, made with five lines, the pentagram.

Then Edith spoke the words they had agreed on: "Demon of the Forbidden Fruit, show yourself." Because he should be listening. After all, if he had left the fruit for Edith to find, it had to be in the hope that she would like the magic and contact him.

And there he was, standing within the pentagram: muscular, naked, with horns, tail and a huge erect phallus. "You called, madam?"

"Oh, put something on!" she said, taken aback.

"Sorry. I drew from the standard format." Suddenly he was in a business suit.

"Thank you. How many questions do I get?"

"As many as you want, madam. There is no limit."

"But don't you want something?"

"Of course. But that can wait until you are satisfied as to my legitimacy."

Edith didn't trust this. He was too accommodating. But she might as well play the game and see what she could learn. "What is your name? Mine's Edith."

"I am Damon. Damon Demon."

"That's nicely alliterative," she said boldly. "Is it really your name, or do you keep it secret so I won't have power over you?"

Damon laughed. "Where I come from, names are fungible, as are bodies. Any will do for spot identification. No power over me."

"Demons do change their bodies," Kent said. "So maybe they change their names too. I'm Kent, by the way."

Damon smiled. "Hi, Kent."

"You say we have no power over you?" Edith asked. "But you came when I conjured you."

"I was expecting your call," Damon explained.

"But you're in the pentagram, so you can't harm us," Edith said.

Damon laughed again. "The figure is merely the site of the image."

"The image?" Kent asked.

"I am not really here, Kent. This is a hologram. You can readily verify this. Touch my body." Damon extended his hand.

Kent was wary. "But if I do, you could grab me and pull me in."

The demon shook his head. "Not so."

"And of course you would lie about it," Kent said.

Damon shook his head. "You are going to have to trust me, if we are to deal."

"What the—heck," Kent said. He reached out to touch the demon's extended hand. But his hand passed right through Damon's hand.

"As you see," Damon said. "I am not physically here. This is a holo image that facilitates our communication. That is all."

"Then where are you?" Edith asked.

Damon looked at her. "I am in my home realm of Lusion. I can't leave it. Only my projection."

"But we conjured you!"

"You requested my appearance. I obliged," the demon explained patiently. "I cannot come here on my own."

She remained suspicious. "Why not?"

"Because this is the mortal realm, and I am not mortal. I have no soul. So I am not real."

"You look and sound real," Kent said.

Damon looked at him. "You have tried the flowers?"

"Yes, of course."

"Is their magic real?"

Kent paused. "In a manner. But it doesn't last."

"And what we do magically gets undone when the magic fades," Edith said.

"So it seems real but isn't," Damon said. "That plant is native to Lusion, as I am. Do you see the parallel?"

"Oh, my," Edith said.

"I, too, am temporary, in your mortal realm," Damon said. "Our present contact will be broken when the magic of this flower fades."

Edith and Kent exchanged a glance. The demon was making sense. "You planted that fruit for a reason," Edith said to Damon.

"Of course I did. Now we can discuss terms. You want permanent magic, right?" They both nodded. "I want a soul." Both froze.

Damon smiled. "Don't look so shocked. You knew I would want that when you called me. Now we need to bargain for a fair trade."

"According to legend and religion," Kent said, "A soul is invaluable."

"So is magic," Damon said. "But perhaps I should clarify."

"Perhaps you should," Edith said grimly. "Isn't

the soul the seat of goodness, decency, compassion, conscience, empathy, and love?"

"No. Folk with souls are not necessarily any more noble than those without. All mortals have souls, but many are evil creatures."

"Then why should we value our souls?" she asked.

"Because they are the seat of reality," Damon said. "You two are real. I am not."

"Do you mean to say that if I lost my soul, I would cease to exist?" Edith asked, appalled.

"Not exactly," Damon said. "I exist."

"But you just said you are not real."

"Exactly. I am not real in the mortal realm, but I do exist in the imaginary realm, Lusion."

"I am having trouble understanding the distinction. Either you exist or you don't."

"That is the fallacy of either-or thinking."

"You can't exist indeterminately!"

"Yes I can. I do. I exist only in Lusion, not in the mortal realm. That's why I want a soul."

"You are imaginary," Kent said. "We are real. But if you get my soul, I'll become imaginary and you'll get real?"

"Exactly."

"Why in heaven would we ever want to do that?" Edith asked. "To commit suicide?"

"No," Damon said. "To transfer to Lusion."

"It doesn't seem like much of a bargain to me," Kent said. "You get life. We get death."

"No. You get a better life. With magic."

"I am not seeing the advantage," Edith said.

"That is why the standard protocol establishes a trial visit before commitment."

"A visit to Lusion?" Kent asked. "To see whether we like it?"

"Exactly," Damon said. "If you don't like it, there is no deal."

"Isn't that like letting the genie out of the bottle?" Edith asked. "And you can't put him in again? How would we get back out?"

"No," Damon said. "You will get a trial visit of a day and night. Twenty four hours, and return automatically at the expiration."

"How can we believe you?" Kent asked. "You'll say anything to trick us into going, and then it will be too late."

Damon sighed. "I know demons have a bad reputation, fostered by lies the religions tell. But you can believe me. Lying is not permitted."

"Why not?" Edith asked.

"Because anyone who goes to Lusion because of a lie will have an agenda of retaliation. That's mischief."

Edith and Kent exchanged another glance. "Say we decide to visit Lusion. That's two of us. What about our situations here?"

"You would need to exchange with two of us," Damon said. "We would borrow your mortal bodies during your absence."

"And do what with them?" Kent asked suspiciously. "Nothing," Damon said. "We would merely assume your lives so that no others knew."

Edith was increasingly curious about the magic realm of Lusion. "You are assuming that if we visit there for a day and night, we will want to move there permanently? And let you keep our bodies and souls?"

"That is my assumption, yes," Damon said.

She looked at Kent. "This is crazy, but I think I want to do it. For a day and night only. A wild gamble, but exciting. You?"

"I'm in," Kent agreed. "What can we lose, but our dull lives?"

"Excellent," Damon said. "I shall summon my girlfriend, Della."

A sultry nude demoness with horns, tail, voluminous red hair, and a huge pair of breasts appeared beside him. "You called, lover?"

"We have a twenty four hour exchange deal. Put something on."

"Sorry." Della became modestly dressed, but still voluptuous.

"Is there a contract to sign in blood, or something?" Kent asked.

"Not at this time," Damon said. "This is a free sample."

"Just like that?" Edith asked. "We can go now?"

"Just like that," Damon agreed. "You will be far better informed when you return."

"Then let's do it," Kent said, taking Edith's hand. Together they stepped into the pentagram, meeting the two demons.

And they were in a nice pavilion, facing a handsome young man and a lovely young woman. "Welcome, honored guests!" the man said.

"You were expecting us?" Edith asked, surprised.

"You are demons?" Kent asked almost at the same time.

"Yes and yes," the girl said.

"We are your host and hostess for your visit, unless you prefer others," the man said. "I am Deron, and this creature is Dulce."

"We are demons," Dulce said. "As are all residents of Lusion. This is by definition, as we have no souls. But we are nice people."

"We watched Damon and Della make contact," Deron said. "So we are familiar with your situation. We will make you comfortable."

"And we certainly hope that you decide to come to Lusion to stay," Dulce said warmly, flashing a brilliant smile at Kent.

Kent was obviously impressed by the smile, buttressed as it was by some cleavage, but he fought back. "What do you stand to gain? Not our souls, as those are already committed, assuming we decide to give them up."

Dulce smiled again. "But you still have them. That lends you special allure. We want to get close to you."

"My soul makes a difference?" Edith asked.

"Yes it does," Deron said. "It is more potent than sex appeal. We all long for souls, and exist for the day when we can recover them and return to mortality."

Edith laughed uneasily. "I have no sex appeal."

"You are mistaken," Deron said. "You now have the power to alter your outer form."

"I suppose I do," Edith agreed. "We can do magic here, regardless of the flower."

"And external forms are meaningless," Deron said.

"We maintain them largely as indications of identity," Dulce said. She shifted to several different forms, including one animal.

"As you can readily do also," Deron said. "But now let us show you around and answer your questions." He reached and took her hand. Dulce did the same with Kent, flashing him another slice of cleavage. Edith concealed her annoyance. It was good to have guides.

The pavilion was in a field of pretty flowers. They walked along a pleasantly winding path to a rippling stream in a quiet forest.

"Someone must spend a lot of time maintaining these premises," Edith said.

"By no means," Deron said. "This is all illusion."

"All illusion!"

"We like to make a good impression," Dulce said. "Illusion is all we have, aside from diversion and companionship."

They emerged from the woods to discover a splendid scene as beautiful as a painting, with snow-capped mountains in the background. In the foreground was a classic castle, girt by turrets and pennants. "This is where you may stay, if you choose," Deron said.

"The cuisine is excellent and plentiful," Dulce said.

"You eat here?" Edith asked. "Why do you need to, if this is all imaginary?"

"We don't need to, physically," Dulce said. "But we enjoy it, and we can't get fat."

"Can't get fat," Edith echoed thoughtfully.

The interior of the castle was like a palace, with bright carpeting, statuary, interior trees, fountains, and spiral escalators.

"We'll show you to your honeymoon suite," Dulce said. "You will want to change so you can enjoy the beach."

"Oh, we're not—"

"It's just the name of the suite," Deron said. "Nothing but the best for our honored guests." Edith and Kent decided not to argue.

The escalator wound up through the ceiling, past layered floors, and into the sky, now circling a tall tower with a panoramic view.

Now Edith saw that the mountains were on one side of the castle, and the ocean beach on the other, with a nice maze garden between.

"Look at that surf!" Kent exclaimed.

"Yes, the waves are continuous," Deron said. "You'll like them. I ride them all the time."

Edith knew nothing about surfing, but could see that Kent was excited. These folk really knew how to turn a young visitor on.

That made her slightly uncomfortable. Their souls evidently made them special, but what about when they lost them? What then?

They reached the Honeymoon Suite. It was at the very pinnacle, about fifty stories up. The extreme height made Edith nervous.

"Try Eden," Kent said. "She's more into adventure."

"She is," Edith said, and changed. "I am," Eden agreed. "I love this."

Then she turned to the others. "This is my other identity. Kent and I need some alone time."

Deron and Dulce literally vanished.

"Things are easy here," Kent said, impressed. "Now that we're alone—" She cut him off with a kiss, and they went on from there. After which ellipsis they admired the lovely suite, donned the bathing suits they found laid out for them, and stepped outside.

Deron and Dulce were waiting at the suite entrance. The four stepped onto the down escalator and spiraled rapidly to the ground.

The beach was sunny and warm, and not at all crowded. "Why so few people here?" Kent asked.

"There are many pleasures," Deron said.

Edith wondered whether that was an evasive answer. But they were already heading into the water. That was pleasure enough for now. She also noticed that all the swimmers and sunbathers were young and beautiful, male and female, just as she herself was. And of course that explained it: if all the people here could assume any forms they wanted, why would any of them be old or ugly?

Kent and Deron quickly took up boards and swam out to where the waves were rising. That left Edith swimming with Dulce.

"You seem pensive," Dulce said. "If swimming

is not to your taste, is there anything else you would rather be doing right now?"

"Not really," Edith demurred.

"Because we have an amusement park, thrill rides, shows, skiing, flower gardens, libraries—"

"What I really want is information," Edith said more boldly than she had meant to. "All this is nice, but where's the catch?"

"Everything is as represented," Dulce said. "You are free to do anything you want, without limit, and nothing you don't want."

"You mentioned gourmet cuisine. Who prepares it? Who serves it? Who washes the dishes? Who takes out the garbage? New recruits?"

"You think there's an underclass? There is not. Nobody does those chores. Everything is done by magic. The magic of imagination."

Edith shook her head.

"I have trouble believing that. I could not even imagine a true gourmet dish; I don't know the recipe."

"Then you must meet our head chef. This way." Dulce swam smoothly for the beach. Edith hesitated, glancing nervously back for Kent.

He was on his board, surfing on a huge rolling wave, sliding down its slope as if it were a snowy hill. He looked thrilled. No help there. Edith decided to play along for now. She followed Dulce to the beach, across it, to the castle, and to the kitchen.

In a moment they were before a large smiling man. "You have a complaint about the food or service, Dulce?" he asked jovially.

"Chef, our guest Eden wants to know about the hired help. Who scrubs the pots?"

Chef laughed. "No one scrubs anything!" he said.

"Oh come on now," Edith said, nettled. "Someone has to peel the potatoes, make the salad, dump the garbage, clean the dishes."

"You forget, honored guest, that you are in Lusion," Chef said. "Everything here is imagined. The only challenge is in the quality of the imagination. I was a top chef back in the mortal realm. I know every detail. I make it so by imagining it. When the guests are done, I banish the remnants. My patrons like it because my imagination in this respect is superior to theirs. I love this job!"

Edith was amazed. "No one does any brute-work? It's all fake?"

"It's all imagined," Dulce said. "Just like your body, and mine."

"Including the castle and the environs," Chef said. "All that is real are our assorted immortal spirits. Which is all that counts."

"But it seems so solid!" Edith protested, pinching her own arm.

"We imagine it well," Chef said. "We have a

good castle man."

"This takes some getting used to," Edith said.

"It does," Dulce said. "But once you acquire the ability to accept it, it's fine."

"This still bothers me," Edith said. "If it is so great here in Lusion, why does anyone ever want to leave? Like Damon and Della."

"Some of us get tired of the spiritual existence," Dulce said. "We want to be able to make a difference. That requires mortality."

"But as mortals you know you will die!"

"But we die making a difference," Dulce said as she led the way back to the beach.

Edith decided not to argue that case. Some folk did give up their lives for a cause. But she wasn't sure she wanted to, herself.

Kent had finished his surfing and was wading to the beach. He evidently hadn't missed her. "Those waves are the greatest!" he said.

"I'm sure," she agreed. "Let's change for dinner. I want to try their food." To see how real it actually seemed when eaten.

"Sure," he agreed amicably.

"Can we change here?"

"You can," Deron said behind him. "Just will yourself to be in a formal outfit."

Kent focused, and his suit became a tuxedo. "Great!"

So Edith focused, and put herself into a strapless gown only Eden could wear.

He put out his elbow. "Shall we go?"

"We shall."

She took his arm. Together they accompanied Deron and Dulce to the chamber.

The dinner was absolutely scrumptious, a virtual banquet. Edith stuffed herself, yet somehow did not become uncomfortably full. But more important, she was not too subtly testing the Chef's imagination, as well as verifying the actual taste of the entries. Her requests were culled from her memory of old comic strips, fairy tales, and childhood imagination topped with egregious puns.

She ordered Roast Rump of Tree-Dwelling Elephant with Ecstasy Sauce, Lunar Escargot, Raga-Muffins, and Green Holy Cowslip Wine. For dessert she had Sinfully Rich Chocolate Mousse Cheesecake with Cruelly Whipped Cream and Unrequited Passion Fruit topping. Lithuanian Loquat Liquor to savor in conclusion.

Meanwhile Kent settled for a hamburger, fries, catsup, and garden-variety beer.

All of it was absolutely delicious, and tasted exactly the way her invented entries should. That Chef was really good. "You win."

Chef appeared by the table. "Thank you. It was a pleasant challenge. Unlike some." He glanced darkly at Kent, who was oblivious.

Deron and Dulce, at an adjacent table, smiled. They had surely seen this sort of thing before. Their own entrees were modest.

After the meal, their guides took them out on the town. They rode in a sport car whose make awed Kent, though Edith drew a blank. Kent drove, delighted to tool it around curves. The car accelerated smoothly and powerfully, seeming to have no upper speed limit. It was dusk, and the city lights were appearing, marvelously colored. There was little other traffic. "How come?" Kent asked.

"We are able to get where we're going without driving," Deron said. "We drive only for pleasure, and in time even that palls."

"I'll never get tired of this. What a machine!" They did not argue, but Edith wondered. Why drive at all, if you didn't need to?

A sign appeared before them YACHT CLUB. "Oh, I'd like to try one of those," Kent said, seeing the marina. "But I can't afford it."

"Oh, but you can," Deron said. "Nothing is beyond your aspiration. Drive on in and select a yacht to take on a tour."

"What, now?"

"Indeed now. They are all awaiting your pleasure."

"Wow." Kent cruised along, peering at the

anchored ships. One had a figurehead. He pulled to a stop. "That one. The *Eager Lady*." For the figurehead was a well-endowed bare-breasted mermaid with a piercing gaze.

"An excellent choice," Deron said enthusiastically. Edith exchanged a glance with Dulce, who made half a shrug. Men were like that.

They boarded the yacht and Kent took the helm. Edith wasn't sure how real yachts worked, but this one was made for amateur control. Soon they were coursing rapidly across the darkening sea. The wake made by the ship glowed with pastel-shaded phosphorescence.

They approached another yacht. This one had buxom girls in bikinis scampering around the deck, pursued by a middle aged man. "I wonder whose wish-fulfillment dream that is?" Edith muttered with heavy irony.

"Mine!" Kent and Deron said almost together.

"Why don't we sensible folk go below while the men gawk?" Dulce suggested. Edith was glad to agree. Evidently dreams differed.

Below-decks was spare but comfortable. They sat and sipped lattes as they gazed out a porthole. "A man thinks a harem will fulfill him forever," Edith remarked.

"The way a child thinks that owning a candy store would be eternally great," Dulce agreed, smiling.

"And the poor man thinks that a million dollars will cure all his ills," Edith said.

"Fantasies are fine," Dulce said. "But they need to be tempered by realism."

"What realism is there here in Lusion?"

"That depends on how you see it. When I was mortal..."

That was an invitation. Edith accepted it. "Yes?"

"I was the wife of an abusive alcoholic. I had no economic escape, as he knew."

"I know the type," Edith said sympathetically. "Mine wasn't abusive, but he was a loss, and I divorced him."

"I could not do that."

"Religion?"

"Yes. I believed in Hell, and did not want to go there. Then a demon contacted me and offered me Heaven."

"Lusion!"

"Lusion," Dulce agreed. "I was so desperate that I made the deal without even questioning it. And it turned out better than I may have deserved. I have been happy here. No one can threaten me physically or economically. I am my own mistress. My own Queen."

"With powers beyond those of any earthly queen," Edith said. "Yet—"

"I wonder how the demoness who took my

place handled it?"

"Your abusive husband?"

"Yes. Because she had my body, my mortal situation. She knew what she was getting into. Yet she was glad."

"She must have had mental or emotional resources you lacked," Edith said.

"Yes. I think she was a martial artist." Edith laughed.

"That would do it. She backed him off and made her own life. Still, it seems that you got the better deal."

"It was right for me."

"I'm still not clear why she wanted to leave Lusion. Is making a difference that important?" Dulce nodded.

"To some of us it is."

Edith wasn't satisfied, but was unable to formulate a relevant question. Then she heard Kent calling. "Eden! You must see this!"

They went back deckside. Light was blazing. "It's the evening fireworks display," Deron explained. "Really worth watching."

He was right. It was a phenomenal exhibition, with rockets exploding into multi-hued expanding spheres. Some formed designs. Others formed moving faces. Some faces even smiled. Taken as a whole, it was the best such display Edith had ever witnessed.

Finally it subsided. "You will want to turn in now," Deron said. "Big day tomorrow."

"What is it?" Edith asked.

"A surprise."

"But first, the dance," Dulce said.

"Oops, I forgot," Deron said. She elbowed him. "Well, you're a man. You miss what's important."

"Yeah? You deserve to be spanked, you impertinent maven."

"Only if we both get bare."

"And embarrass our guests? Not right now."

"Chicken." Fun dialogue, but Edith wondered how much of it was staged for their benefit. Their guides were trying almost too hard.

They changed effortlessly for the dance, which was in the castle ballroom. It was billed as informal, so the women were in blouses and double-circle skirts, the men in plaid shirts and jeans. The music was lovely and compelling, played by an enthusiastic band. Edith realized that skilled musicians liked to exercise their trade for an appreciative audience, just as the Chef did. Why not?

Couples moved out. Kent gazed at the dance floor uncertainly. "I'm not sure I know how," he confided. Edith had a similar doubt.

"Be not concerned," Dulce told him. "All you need to do is stand there." She led him onto the floor, took his hand, and spun.

Kent did just stand there awkwardly, but Dulce moved so well around him that it looked as though he were actively participating. She twirled so that her skirt flung out, flashing her fine legs right up to the panties. Then she wrapped his arm around her and leaned back as if being dipped. She held him tightly and turned them both about so that it looked as if he were swinging her. They really were dancing, in their fashion. Edith had to admire the technique, but she was also slightly jealous of its seduction. How close, how long could Kent remain to this lovely young woman without feeling the considerable allure of that flexing body?

Then Deron took Eden by the hand and urged her to the dance floor. "Just follow me," he murmured, taking her firmly in his arms. And they were dancing more competently than Edith had ever danced before. His technique was flawless and tuned to her, making her sparkle like a turning diamond. She twirled, flashing her own thighs. She saw her reflection in a wall mirror. She was lovely! She absolutely loved it. She had never been this graceful or sexy even when she really was 25. She was breathless and exhilarated.

The dance ended and they returned to the sideline. Deron and Dulce brought them cake and punch. "You did well," Deron said.

Both Kent and Edith laughed, knowing that

anything they had done was owed to their expressive partners. "I wish I really could dance like that," Edith said wistfully.

"Oh, you can, once you learn," Deron said. "Magic is great, but some things still do have to be done the old fashioned way, like learning new skills and honing the imagination. But in time you really can do them."

"I did not know how to dance when I came to Lusion," Dulce said. "But I learned. Just as I learned how to flirt and make love."

"And I learned to paint and handle a boat," Deron said. "There is time and opportunity here for anything. Anything at all."

Edith found that very interesting. These folk did not have to work for a living, and could develop artistic skills. She liked that.

Then the music started up again. It was time to dance. They went into it with a will, improving with each one. What a fling!

Hours later, pleasantly exercised, they retired to their lofty suite. "We should make passionate love and go to sleep," Edith said.

"Sounds good to me," Kent agreed. "After dancing with Dulce, I'm thoroughly charged up."

"I have something else in mind," she said.

"Oh, crap! Can it wait until after love and sleep?"

"No, we need to do it now, while they won't be watching us."

"They won't?"

"Because they will be sure we're safely accounted for. They have their own lovemaking and sleeping to do now."

"Yeah."

"So now is the time to sneak out the back way and find out what's really going on with Lusion."

He nodded. "I am hearing you."

"Everything so far has been a show to impress us," she continued. "And they *have* impressed us. But why are they trying so hard?"

"Why indeed," he agreed. "We're just ordinary folk, especially without the magic. What do they really want with us? Fresh meat?"

"Not literally, I think," Edith said. "For one thing, they don't eat. I talked with Dulce, and she comes across as a real person."

"And one sexy dancer," he said appreciatively. "But then what is it? We're just not all that special."

"That is the question."

"That is the question," he echoed seriously. "But you know they won't tell us. How do you figure to find out the real story?"

"By sneaking out the back way and looking behind the facade."

He frowned. "Eden, we're fifty stories high.

There is no back exit."

"You forget the magic. We can fly."

"Well I'll be," he said, surprised. "That's so. But is it safe?"

"If it's not, let's find out."

"We do need to know, either way," he said. "Better to take a fall than be deluded."

"That was my thought," she agreed, grimly.

They turned out the lights as if about to make love and sleep. Then they opened the rear window and floated out. They didn't fall.

It was dark. "Make night vision," Edith said, focusing. Now they could see well enough in the darkness, thanks to the magic.

"Now what?" he whispered. "It looks the same."

Edith was unsure. "I visited Florida once, on a vacation. I discovered that behind the tourist beachfront facade there was a regular city, suburbs, oak and pine trees, and swamp. Ordinary, just like my hometown."

"So let's fly to the Everglades," he said. "Which way?"

Edith considered. "Let's parallel the coast so we don't fly in circles."

They flew above the winding beach. The landscape soon changed, becoming dark and menacing. But she refused to turn back just yet. Then they heard a kind of swishing in the air ahead. "Uh-oh," Kent said. "I think we'd better conjure weapons. Something's coming."

"I don't know how to use a weapon," she protested.

"Can of pepper spray," he suggested. In a moment he had a sword, she a can.

Huge dark shapes loomed close. "Bats!" Edith exclaimed, horrified. She had always foolishly feared them, and these were giants.

The bats circled around them as if considering what to bite off first. She held her can, terrified, ready to spray. Would it work?

"Maybe if we drop down close to the water they won't follow," Kent said, nervous despite his formidable sword.

"Maybe," she agreed.

They dived, plummeting toward the dark sea below. The bats circled, following. Then they saw the big shark fins slicing the waves.

"Maybe the beach," Edith said desperately. They arrowed toward the beach—and saw monstrous crabs sidling along, orienting on them.

"I see a cave!" Kent cried. "This way!" He flew toward it, Edith following. The crabs scuttled after them, huge pincers waving. But they had the advantage of surprise, and zoomed to the cave entrance before the crabs could cut them off. The crabs veered off.

"They're afraid of the cave!" Edith said breathlessly.

"But why?" Kent asked. "I don't trust it. What would scare off a big crab?"

There was a vicious growl from deep within the cave. "A cave bear!" Edith said, horrified.

"And we're trapped here," Kent said.

Then Edith got a flash of genius. "We can change forms! Let's be bears!" Immediately they changed to two hulking surly bears. Not only did that back off the cave bear, it altered their perspective. "Hey, she's a pretty good-looking creature," Kent said.

"Well I should hope so," the lady bear responded. "I worked hard to get it right. To what do I owe the honor of a mortal visit?"

They stared at her, dumbfounded. "You— you're a person!" Edith said.

"A person in a private retreat," the bear agreed. "What else?"

"We were just trying to see the other side of Lusion," Edith said. "To avoid all the showcasing. Then the bats and crabs came."

The bear laughed. "The bats are tame. The crabs are illusion. This is the realm of illusion. Hence its name. You didn't know?"

"Maybe we should have known," Edith said, embarrassed. "We were perhaps a bit, well, paranoid."

"It happens," the bear agreed.

"We apologize for intruding on your retreat," Edith said. She turned to Kent. "I think we should quietly return to our suite."

"We should," Kent agreed. "We've made fools enough of ourselves for one night." They turned around and padded out of the cave.

The crabs were waiting on the beach. Edith nerved herself and approached one. It held its ground. She walked to it—and through it.

It was, indeed, illusion. The cave bear had spoken truly. Then the pair of them flew up into the dark sky. The bats did not attack. They flew back to the turret, and scrambled back inside the suite. Then Edith realized that they were bears. She hastily changed.

"Maybe let's not mention this tomorrow," Kent said, also reverting to human form.

"Let's not," Edith agreed. "We were idiots."

"Now let's make out," he said. She sighed inwardly. He did seem to have a one-track mind. But she didn't want to make a scene.

So they made love, and slept. Or Kent did. Edith lay awake a while, pondering things. Did she really want this? She loved being young and vibrant, but she did not want to be a chronic sex object. And what about Lusion? Even if it was for real, was it for her? But mainly she still had trouble fathoming why the folk of Lusion, who had everything they wanted, literally, wanted mortality. To make a difference, they said. But hardly any one person on Earth really made much of a difference. It was highly unlikely that anyone taking the place of Edith or Kent would accomplish anything spectacular or significant. They were simply too ordinary. So that rationale did not seem sensible. That left her floundering in search of something that did make sense. Where was the catch?

Finally she drifted off to a troubled sleep, wondering in passing why anyone even needed sleep in a realm of pure imagination.

She woke to find Kent kissing her. He wanted more sex. Maybe she shouldn't have let herself sleep in the Eden body. Too late now. But in another half day it would be over, as they returned to mortal Earth. So she obliged him, and actually this body did like it. It was Edith herself who was the old dowdy. And of course she could change that forever, by moving to Lusion. Did she want to? There was the question she couldn't properly answer. Her life as a mortal was pretty much nothing. What did she have to lose?

"I can hardly wait to see what the restaurant has for breakfast," Kent said eagerly. Which was another question. Why bother to eat?

Deron and Dulce were waiting for them outside the door. "Half a day left," Deron said. "Let's make the most of it." Kent nodded.

Dulce took Edith's hand as they rode the escalator down. "You seem pensive, again."

"I just can't make up my mind," Edith said.

"Perhaps today will clarify things. We have a full schedule."

"Perhaps it will," Edith said, feeling as she had with Kent: balked.

It was a delightful breakfast, with every kind of cereal, pastry, eggs, beverages and more. Edith hardly noticed what she ate.

"Now it's time for our surprise," Deron said as they went to the ballroom. "Behold!" And there was a festive array of decorations.

"What is it?" Kent asked. "It' a party," Deron said.

"What's the occasion?"

"Your unbirthdays."

"Our whats?"

"Unbirthdays."

"I don't get it."

"Well, it's not your birthday, so it must be your unbirthday. We are celebrating. There's food, games, gifts."

"You evidently like parties," Edith murmured to Dulce.

"Any pretext will do," Dulce agreed.

"Okay," Kent said, getting into it. "Where are the dancing girls?"

"Right here," Deron said, gesturing to a huge model of a cake. The lid and the sides opened.

A platoon of nearly nude dancing girls emerged, stepping smartly, kicking toward the ceiling.

"For pity's sake," Edith muttered.

"This is not to your taste?" Dulce inquired.

"That's right," Edith said hotly. "If this is all Lusion has to offer, count me out."

"I will make you a deal. Give each of us one hour with each of you to make our case, and then we'll leave you alone. Fair enough?"

"Deal!" Edith agreed gladly.

Dulce caught Deron's eye, then snapped her fingers. The scene froze in place, dancing girls and all.

"This way," Dulce said, walking past a girl in high kick mode, to the entrance. Edith followed, bemused. Lusion had surprises yet!

Outside, they flew up and across the landscape to a distant cliff, then to a truck-sized cave at its base. "Here live the bats."

"The bats!" Edith exclaimed, amazed anew.

"I work with them in my off hours," Dulce explained. "They mostly sleep by day."

"We—we encountered them last night," Edith said, realizing that Dulce probably already knew. "They—they circled around us."

"We have a deal with them," Dulce said. "They keep the castle environs clear of nasty bugs, some of which are huge, and we help safeguard their welfare. They were here before us, and were very useful when we needed advice about Lusion. They signaled us that two visitors were lost. We told them to keep an eye on you, just in case you got into real trouble, knowing you wanted to explore."

So there had never been real danger. "Thank you," Edith said. "For your discretion."

Dulce smiled. "We were all once new here."

They entered the cave. Dozens of man-sized bats were hanging from the cave ceiling, sleeping. Dulce approached one. "This is Bonnie Bat," she said. "She was injured last week in a collision and suffered internal injuries that are not healing well. I do what I can but it's not sufficient. I don't know enough bat physiology, so my touch lasts only two or three days. I wish I could do more."

Edith was touched. This woman was really trying to make a difference, here in Lusion. "Can I help?"

Dulce considered. "You might."

Edith put her hands beside Dulce's on the bat's head and willed Bonnie to be mended. The effect was miraculous. Healing power surged. The bat became vibrant, and Edith knew she was completely well again. "It's the power of your soul!" Dulce said, amazed.

"My soul?"

"You're a visitor. You retain your soul. Not only does that give you magnetic personal appeal, it lends you power."

"The power to heal," Edith said, impressed.

"To make a difference, yes," Dulce said. "As you just did with Bonnie. But I must warn you that if you come here to stay, you will no longer have your soul, and won't be able to perform miracles. You'll be ordinary."

"Ordinary," Edith echoed. "But I could still try to help bats or other animals, in my more limited capacity."

"Yes, as I do."

"I think I would like that. Parties and magic are fine, but this is meaningful."

"This is my case. Now it's Deron's turn with you."

"Deron's turn. Does he have a serious side too?"

"Oh, yes. We all do. Parties are for visitors. Behind the scenes it's serious."

"I was looking for the reality behind the facade," Edith said. "Maybe now I have found it."

"Maybe you have," Dulce agreed. "Yet—"

"There is something else?"

"There is. Kent is more, shall we say, party oriented than you are. His needs are more immediate."

"Amen," Edith agreed.

"So to make my case to him I will not show him bats. Instead it may need to be more direct pleasure."

"Sex galore," Edith agreed.

"If you are amenable. I do not wish to interfere with your relationship."

"Don't worry," Edith said. "Our relationship is mostly one of convenience; we're not really a couple. I found the magic fruit, and we followed up. That's it."

"Then with your tolerance I will show him some of the art and power of sex," Dulce said. "This is what Lusion can offer him."

Edith suspected that Kent's love of Eden was about to transfer to Dulce, who had similar sex appeal buttressed by maturity. That would be convenient. Eden would still be there, but no longer monopolizing his attention. Edith could have her own life.

They returned to the castle, where the party remained frozen. Deron and Kent were returning from another direction. Nice timing.

"Wow!" Kent said. "Deron just showed me the game of Freak Poker. What an experience! I have to play more of that soon as I can!"

"I'm sure Dulce will hold your attention similarly," Deron said.

"I believe I will," Dulce said, taking his hand. "This way, stud."

Deron looked at Edith. "If you care to come admire my etchings?"

"By all means," she agreed, curious about his serious side.

He led her to his room, which turned out to be like a small gallery featuring pictures of a ferocious large fish. That was curious. "This is a mosasaur," Deron said, seeing her glance. "A formidable carnivorous lizard of the Cretaceous Period, sixty million years ago."

"But it's a fish!" Edith protested.

"No, it's a marine lizard the size of a small whale. I am studying for my PhD in Mosasaur Evolution."

"But that's obscure!"

"Indeed. But I need to write my doctoral thesis on something not done before. This qualifies."

"There are doctorates here?"

"Not exactly. But I will research and write my thesis, and others will judge whether it suffices."

"For the satisfaction?"

"And the knowledge. I am genuinely interested in the Age of Dinosaurs that preceded the Age of Mammals."

Edith was impressed. There was indeed significant substance here. "How does this make the case that I should come here to stay?"

"I crave a favor that only you can grant. The Lusion Library's physically imaginary, but its information is real. But it's dated."

"I see the problem."

"It gets updated by new arrivals from more

recent times. I understand there is now the Internet."

"There is."

"If you could look up Mosasaur there, that information would be in your mind when you came here. If you decide to return here."

"So you could complete your research!" she said.

"Yes. If you return."

"If I return," she said. "And if I don't?"

"I'll miss you."

"That's all? No special inducements?"

"None," he said. "I think you now know enough of Lusion to make a sensible decision."

"No promises of endless parties? Phenomenal sex? Wonderful games?"

He shook his head. "Those are ornaments. You don't need them."

"Give me one good reason why I should come to Lusion to stay."

"Only if you truly want to, otherwise you're better off mortal."

"Why should I pass up all the remarkable entertainments here?"

"Because they can get dull. They are temporary, not permanent."

"You are telling me to stay in my dull mortal existence?"

"Edith, you have a mind and conscience. You

can make a difference."

"I don't see how."

"When you leave here, see what Della is doing. That should show you a way. What she can do, you can do."

"If I return here, I'll be immortal. There I will eventually die."

He laughed. "Immortality is overrated. When you have indulged yourself in every conceivable way a hundred times, you can lose your taste for indulgence. That's not a problem for a mortal."

"I'm curious. How old are you?"

"Age is meaningless here, since you can change to any age you prefer."

"How old?" she repeated.

"You would reckon it nine hundred and forty two years."

"And Dulce?"

"She's a bit younger. Only seven hundred and some years."

Edith digested that. These people truly were immortal. And they didn't care about it? Hard to believe! "Let's return to the party."

They walked to the ballroom, where the festivities were frozen in place. The dancers were still kicking high, showing their all.

Kent and Dulce arrived from the other direction. He looked dazed, ignoring the lifted legs.

He must have seen something better.

He spied Edith. "Let's dance, Eden," he said.

So they danced, to the restored music. "There's something on your mind?" she asked.

"Oh yes! I want to move to Lusion. You can stay mortal if you want."

"You would go without me?"

He paused briefly. She knew why. "Now don't take this the wrong way, Eden, but—"

"Don't be concerned," she said. "I told Dulce it was all right."

"She's the one!"

Just so. "We're not a couple," she said. "Just two people working together to explore new prospects. I'm still considering mine."

"Good enough." It was clear that his love for Eden had been preempted by a greater love. Dulce had been professionally persuasive. So Kent had decided.

Edith remained uncertain. She was impressed by both Dulce and Deron, and by Lusion itself. But was that all? She still feared a catch. Until she figured that out, she lacked information to make an informed decision. What was she missing?

They finished the dance, and Kent went on to dance with Dulce. Deron joined Edith. "If still in doubt, stay mortal," he advised.

"What side are you on?" she flared. "Aren't you supposed to persuade me to come here to Lusion so someone else can have my soul?"

"Edith, you are a sensible woman, and I would love to have your company for an indefinite period," he said seriously. "But—"

"But I'm ordinary. I'm not the shadow of Dulce."

He took her hand. "Stop that. You're not the shadow of the woman you will be in another century. I relish the thought of being your friend and your lover as you mature, and I think you would like me too."

"You can't be serious!"

"Assume your natural form."

Bemused, she did: slightly dowdy, more than slightly overweight, some lines.

"And here is my appearance at fifty," he said. He became a portly man with receding hair, slightly warped nose, and crooked teeth.

Then he kissed her. Physically it was nothing special, but emotionally it was a paean of desperate desire. He did indeed want her.

Oh. It was her soul that turned him on. "If I come here, I won't have my soul," she reminded him.

"True. So this is no clincher."

"So what do I have to recommend me?" Because now, perversely, she wanted to be persuaded.

"Dulce was no beauty either, initially."

"Magic transformed her," Edith agreed, privately satisfied with this information.

"But she quickly learned the arts, as you will."

"So if I come here to stay," she said, "I will be immortal, have powers of magic limited only by my imagination, and sex/romance."

"That's it," he agreed. "Della will have your mortal life, and I will have your company. It's a reasonably fair trade, overall."

"Why aren't *you* trying to become mortal, to make a difference?"

"I am from a different age. I would not be comfortable there."

"Well, I'll think about it." It did seem to be a fair trade, for those who wanted it. Was she one of them? She just didn't know.

The party continued, seemingly unaware of the two hour freeze. Kent was obviously having a good time, but Edith was torn by doubt.

Then seemingly suddenly it was time to return; their 24 hours was expiring. The pavilion was unchanged.

Kent kissed Dulce ardently.

Edith shook Deron's hand. "Thank you for your guidance," she said. "I'm sorry I am as yet unable to give you a definite answer."

"If you return, I will welcome you," he said. "But you must honestly judge what is best for you. Only then can you be satisfied."

They stepped into the pentagram. They were

back in her apartment.

"You will have a day to decide," Damon's voice came from behind.

They turned. There were Damon and Della in the pentagram. "Some things you need to know before the magic fades," Damon said. "I've found a job for you, Kent. It's lowly clerical, but has prospects for the future."

"I don't want it," Kent said. "Keep it."

"I will, gladly," Damon said. "But protocol requires that twenty four hour wait."

"And what of you, Della?" Edith asked.

"You will find the pots I have set up to grow new plants when the new fruits develop. And you will see the novel I have started."

"Novel?" Edith asked blankly. "Your mortal body has a fair talent for imagination. I am using it to write a novel about Lusion."

"But why?"

"To acquaint more people with the concept, so that when they encounter the fruits they will be ready to visit there."

It struck Edith like a blinding light. "You really do mean to make a difference!"

"Yes, of course. That's why I came here."

"Invoke us again tomorrow when the last flower blooms," Damon said.

"If you want to go to Lusion to stay," Della

said. They faded.

"I'm going there," Kent said. "Dulce's the one for me." Edith wondered whether he knew how old Dulce was, but it didn't matter.

"Tomorrow," she said.

"You bet." He departed. He had never questioned her own decision. Again, it didn't matter; he could go alone.

The pots were there, and the manuscript started on the computer. "Gloria knew the moment she saw it that this was forbidden fruit." Edith smiled. Far more dramatic than her own discovery of the fruit. "Yet it appealed to her strangely." Oh, yes. This might do.

The fruit had led her to Lusion. Was that properly Illusion, or Delusion? Immortality, youth, indulgence. So it was all imaginary. What did this dull mortal life have to offer her except boredom and eventual death? Why not escape into the realm of imagination?

Then she remembered the requests of their guides. She connected to the Internet and soon was scanning the Physiology of Bats, and the Evolution of the Cretaceous Mosasaur. She knew then that she would go to Lusion. She could make a difference there, ironically. She did not understand much if any of the technical information she was garnering, but trusted that Dulce and Deron would.

Now at last she could relax. She had made her decision, for good or ill. Right or wrong, she would be satisfied. She was choosing adventure over commonplace, and her soul was not too great a price to pay. She was satisfied that her body and soul would endure.

Kent came promptly and eagerly next afternoon. Now Edith was excited too. The flower bloomed, they sniffed, and summoned the demons.

"We're ready," Kent said.

"Thank you," Della said. Edith realized that the demons, too, had been worried about the decision.

They stepped into the demons, making the exchange. And were in the pavilion.

Deron and Dulce were waiting, smiling, relieved. Deron enfolded Edith, and Dulce melted into Kent. "I did my very best to provide you a proper basis for decision," Deron said. "But I very much wanted you to come."

"I researched Mosasaur," she said.

"That too, he said, and kissed her. "Now let's make love."

"What, here? In this body?" Because she hadn't changed to Eden.

"Why not? We're alone." For Kent and Dulce had disappeared.

Then they were doing it and she was loving it. Bodies didn't matter here. At least not their appearance. Preference was all, here.

The following weeks were a whirl of fun. Deron was highly pleased with the research she had done, and so was Dulce. And the bats.

And suddenly it was the one year anniversary of their arrival in Lusion. Naturally there was a big party. There was always a party.

Kent approached her. "I feel guilty," he said.

"Why?"

"Dulce has been absolutely great. She's perfect. But I am missing reality."

Edith felt a chill. She had a similar concern. "Immortality and magic and sex are not enough," she said.

"Not enough," he agreed.

"Because in the end, existence here doesn't make a difference," she said.

"That's it," he agreed. "I never believed it, before."

"So what do we do now?" she asked.

He considered. "I guess we tell Deron and Dulce. They've probably encountered this before."

"Probably," she agreed. So they went to Deron and Dulce and explained.

"Yes," Deron said. "We had hoped you would be content."

"But those with minds tend not to be," Dulce said sadly. "They tend to crave more challenge than

Lusion provides. We do understand."

"That was the case with Damon and Della," Edith said.

"And many others," Deron agreed. "Folk have to experience complete license in order to comprehend its ultimate futility."

"And you," Kent asked. "Why are you satisfied to remain forever in Lusion?"

"We are not," Dulce said. "But someone has to stay here to maintain the essential framework. The castle, the deal with the bats."

"Otherwise it would all dissolve," Deron said. "There would be chaos, as there was before us. That would ruin it as a retreat."

"You would rather be mortal?" Edith asked.

"Oh yes," Deron said. "To make a difference."

"But you are making a difference here!"

"This is impermanent."

"No it isn't," Edith said hotly. "You are making it possible for others to return to make a difference."

"That's second hand."

"The hell it is! You're a key link in the chain. Without you it would fall apart. That's a huge difference."

Deron shrugged. "Regardless, this is the nature of our contribution to the effort. Until such time as others take our places."

Edith suffered another revelation. "I want to

do it too! Not to replace you. To help you make the difference. Your role is worthy."

"You are welcome," Deron said. "I am gratified."

Dulce looked at Kent. "And you?"

"I am torn," he said candidly. "Edith makes a good case. I've done nothing with my life so far, just lived it up. My life as a mortal made no more real difference than this."

"But you could change," Dulce pointed out. "As others who have come here have done."

"And I could help others change," Kent said. "As you have been helping me change, Dulce. I suspect it has been a real chore at times."

"I would not say that," she protested.

"And you can teach me how not to say it to the next ignorant visitors to Lusion. To have your great patience and discretion."

"If it is your true desire," Dulce agreed.

"I think it is. I don't need to search elsewhere for meaning. I can find it right here."

"As you wish," Deron said, smiling. "You are free to change your minds at any time. Meanwhile, welcome to the responsibility."

Edith exchanged a glance with Kent. It seemed the two of them had finally found their mission, where they had least expected it.

AUTHOR'S NOTE

This concludes Tweet Story #5, "Forbidden Fruit." Those who are tired of spinning their wheels in this mortal life are welcome to be alert for strange magic fruit. There are "demons" who will be happy to take your places as you visit Lusion. Meanwhile you are free to enter the realm of imagination at any time, without risking your mortality, as you have done while reading this novelette-length piece. It won't make a difference in the real world, but does that really matter? More power to you!

This book was proofread by Scott M Ryan and Anne White, who caught the frequent errors my own editing missed. Readers who want to know more of me can find me at my website www.HiPiers.com.

ABOUT THE AUTHOR

Piers Anthony is one of the world's most prolific and popular authors. His fantasy Xanth novels have been read and loved by millions of readers around the world, and have been on the *New York Times* Best Seller list many times. Although Piers is mostly known for fantasy and science fiction, he has written several novels in other genres as well, including historical fiction, martial arts, and horror. Piers lives with his wife of 60 years in a secluded woods hidden deep in Central Florida.

Piers Anthony's official website is HI PIERS at www.hipiers.com, where he publishes his monthly online newsletter. HI PIERS also has a section reviewing many of the online publishers and self-publishing companies for your reference if you are looking for a non-traditional solution to publish your book.

Printed in Great Britain
by Amazon

25752314R00088